ÖPIE JONES
AND THE SUPERHERO SLUG

First published in Great Britain in 2022 by Farshore

An imprint of HarperCollins*Publishers*
1 London Bridge Street, London SE1 9GF

farshore.co.uk

HarperCollins*Publishers*
1st Floor, Watermarque Building,
Ringsend Road Dublin 4, Ireland

Text copyright © 2022 Nat Luurtsema
Illustrations © 2022 Fay Austin

The moral rights of the author and illustrator have been asserted.
A CIP catalogue record for this title is available from the British Library

ISBN 978 1 4052 9610 6
Printed and bound in the UK using 100% renewable electricity
at CPI Group (UK) Ltd
1

Stay safe online. Any website addresses listed in this book are
correct at the time of going to print. However, Farshore is not
responsible for content hosted by third parties. Please be aware
that online content can be subject to change and websites can
contain content that is unsuitable for children. We advise that
all children are supervised when using the internet.

MIX
Paper from
responsible sources
FSC™ C007454
www.fsc.org

This book is produced from independently certified FSC™ paper
to ensure responsible forest management.

For more information visit: www.harpercollins.co.uk/green

"I LIKE BOOKS THAT START WITH QUOTATIONS, SOMETHING INSPIRING. LOT OF PRESSURE, THOUGH. UM. OK, I'VE GOT A GOOD ONE.

CABBAGE IS A MORE EXCITING VEGETABLE THAN PEOPLE REALISE."

POSTOFF THE SLUG

I am aware I'm a little grumpy in this book. But you need to understand, I was chilly and it affected my mood.

I know, I know . . . last time I was too hot and that made me moody.

There's a specific temperature at which I'm happy.

I'm not often at that temperature.

CHAPTER ONE

OPIE MASSAGED HER HEAD AND BREATHED DEEPLY. She was having a Difficult Thursday morning.

Sure, you may think, I've had one of them. None of my socks match, I can't get a comb through my hair, barely a smudge of toothpaste left in the tube. And, while I have sympathy for you, Opie was not having one of *those* bad mornings. She was having a weirder one.

Opie was standing in the cold, dark expanse of her school gym. It was seven thirty in the morning, she was tired and having a silent argument with a large group of beetles. She was communicating with them telepathically because Opie was an animal mind reader.

How exciting, you might think. Yeah, sometimes. Not right now.

These beetles were a species known as wood-boring beetles. And they were living up to their name by being very boring.

One of the beetles was larger and bossier than the rest and he was leading the conversation. He rolled over on to one side and scratched his belly with a lazy leg.

MOST BOSSY BEETLE

The thing is. I don't mean to be patronising, old fruit, but the average House Longhorn Beetle –

One of his friends snickered.

ANOTHER BEETLE

I wouldn't call yourself "average", being a little modest there.

A DIFFERENT BEETLE

Well, quite!

YET ANOTHER BEETLE

I was about to say the same thing...

MOST BOSSY BEETLE

You're far too kind.

Opie picked a scratchy piece of sleep from the corner of her eye and wished she was somewhere else.

MOST BOSSY BEETLE

But my point is, young lady, that we as a species enjoy a moister wood, ideally damp plywood.

YET ANOTHER BEETLE

So yummy.

MOST BOSSY BEETLE

So who would believe us when we dash out of the old, dry woodwork at your school making yummy noises? "Oooh delightful, a crumbly bit of door, my favourite!"

The other beetles chuckled and Opie smiled politely, thinking that she must be the least glamorous superhero in the world.

About a year ago she had discovered that she could read animals' minds. She had been hearing strange conversations nibbling away at the edge of her mind for a few months until she realised she was actually hearing the thoughts of animals.

It was AMAZING to then be recruited into The Resistance, a gang of mind readers determined to thwart the plans of a billionaire called Varling who was using all the other mind readers in the country to make himself richer and everyone less happy.

Thwart. What a great word.

Opie loved being part of The Resistance, even if the other mind readers teased her because they heard human thoughts and she was the only one dealing with animal thoughts.

But she was their best hope for thwarting Varling's plan to buy Opie's school, Saint Francis, and turn it into a warehouse. Last term his team of mind readers had been targeting Saint Francis students and making them fight each other until almost half the school was excluded. At which point he planned to demand that this "dangerous" school be closed down so he could buy the building.

His plan had been working. But one day on the way to school, Opie had struck up a conversation with a slug staging an impressive heist on a tomato plant. He was easy to talk to, and she found herself confiding in him about her problems.

The Slug had once spent a week stuck to the window of a house for sale, and he had learned that before you buy a property, you had to have a surveyor come round to tell you if there was anything wrong with it. Some problems were so serious they could stop the sale of a building.

One of those problems was woodworm . . .

The Slug had turned to Opie and waggled his eye stalks slowly and meaningfully at her. Then he got dizzy and stopped. But she had understood.

Opie had assembled a team of wood-boring beetles and brought them to her school to stage a woodworm infestation. It was definitely working. She had seen several teams of men in yellow hard hats come to the school and stare seriously at door frames.

Her parents, Harvey and Violet, were both actors, and thanks to them she knew the best way to coax a good performance out of her beetles. It was called the Criticism Sandwich.

1. Compliment (*"I love what you're doing, great energy!"*)

2. Criticism (*"Could you stop swinging your arms all over the place? You're hitting the other actors!"*)

3. And then, to close the sandwich, one more compliment (*"You have such a nice voice that if I called 999 and you were the operator, I would forget my emergency and just want to chat."*)

The Criticism Sandwich had backfired, and the beetles had become horribly arrogant about their talents. Opie now had to spend most mornings in the gym listening to their complaints about the job. Today they were adamant that "the audience" wouldn't believe they'd want to eat a dry old school.

OPIE
You're eating a bit right now.

Looking guilty, Another Beetle hid a shard of wood under his wing. A Different Beetle glared at him.

OPIE

Also – sorry, I feel like we have been over this – can you not *actually* eat the school, please? The whole point is I want to stay here and get an education, not have it collapse around my ears. This is pretend. The surveyors just have to *see* you, OK?

YET ANOTHER BEETLE

Oh, right, right . . . no, you did say. I forgot.

OPIE

I have to go, I'll be late for assembly. You're doing a great job, um . . . fantastic energy.

Opie hurried out of the gym and towards the school hall, rubbing her dry, tired eyes. There was a little gentle squirming in the top pocket of her dungarees, and The Slug poked his head out.

THE SLUG

You dealt with that very well, Opes.

Opie smiled at him and gently patted her pocket. Ideally, she would have a less gooey sidekick, but The Slug was so sensible and encouraging, so much better than her first attempt at a sidekick: her neighbour's cat Margot.

Margot was deliberately unhelpful because she found it funny when things went wrong. That attitude made a superhero's work harder than it needed to be. Batman would never put up with it.

THE SLUG

Time check. Two minutes to assembly.

Opie started running and made it through the doors just in time to slip into a seat next to her best friend Jackson.

Jackson was charming, funny and absent-minded. He often came to school in his slippers. But he was so popular that he never got teased. "A heart of gold," Opie had overheard her French teacher, Monsieur Lunarca, say. "A head of marshmallows."

On the other side of Jackson was Cillian, who was

not so sweet but a lot smarter. He had been Jackson's friend since primary school and did not enjoy sharing him with Opie, who had only moved to the school a year and a half ago.

Luckily, he didn't keep his feelings to himself, but let them out in spiteful remarks. Much healthier.

They had a scratchy relationship, but over the past few months Opie had grown fond of Cillian and she thought he felt the same, though he'd never admit it. She had given him a friendship bracelet last term and once saw the edge of it poking out from his sleeve, although he had tucked it away quickly and never mentioned it.

"Do you smell *slug*?" Cillian mouthed to Jackson and Opie, acting concerned, when he knew full well that there was a slug nearby – and also that slugs did not smell.

"No," Opie whispered firmly, earning herself a shush from their form teacher Ms Mollo. Really, was that fair when she was defending the feelings of a friend? No, she thought. It was not.

Ms Boutros, their head teacher, was not reading

the usual announcements to start assembly. ("Someone has dropped a phone. But, as you're not meant to have phones in school, we can organise your detention when you come and collect it.") Today, Ms Boutros was telling the school that unfortunately they were going to have to close for the next two weeks.

Opie did a wide-eyed "Oh no!" face at Jackson and Cillian. Did this mean that Varling had bought the school?

"Unfortunately, the school has a woodworm problem," Ms Boutros continued. "A structural engineer said that our gym had been nibbled so much it was 'like a Crunchie bar without the chocolate'."

"Oooh I could go for a Crunchie . . ." said a small voice within the Year 5s. Ms Mollo shushed him too. She was like that when she hadn't had her morning coffee.

Opie grimaced. Those beetles had really gone Method with their acting. Why couldn't they just pretend? She had clearly found the most melodramatic insects in the wood.

She could feel Cillian's eyes boring into her, so she pretended to be fascinated by a small hole on the knee of her dungarees. *Great plan, Opie, really well done*, she thought. She was not looking forward to telling The Resistance that she had actually managed to shut her school down, and basically helped Varling. She might as well switch sides.

"But," said Ms Boutros. Opie looked up, hearing a smile in her voice. "You will definitely be coming back in two weeks. We all will. To *our* school."

She wasn't talking to the pupils sat on the floor but to the teachers sat around the edge of the room, who all exchanged secretive smiles.

Opie straightened up and looked at her friends. Cillian raised his eyebrows. Jackson mouthed "What?" He was always about ten minutes behind what was going on. But Cillian wasn't. He had understood immediately. Varling wasn't going to buy their school! That's what Ms Boutros meant.

Opie couldn't wait to tell The Resistance. They had thwarted evil, again! *Such* a good word.

This is a lovely derelict building, we've been here about a year now? Nice community spirit, we even have a little garden out front, full of dandelions. Lovely.

The biggest plus about this place, it's got no wood-boring beetles. Those guys are not great flatmates. I don't wanna be mean, we're a welcoming collective, but they really will bang on about themselves for hours. Creates a very uncool vibe.

So, yeah, we're lucky to have none of them. Touch wood. Pardon the pun, ha ha.

CHAPTER TWO

OPIE HURRIED BACK TO THE GYM AS SOON AS assembly was over. She had to tell the beetles that their acting had done the trick and, most importantly, get them out of the way before exterminators were brought in.

She darted past a line of smaller kids dragging their PE bags behind them as they dawdled to their gym class. At the speed they were moving, she had a good couple of minutes to skid into the gym, scoop up the beetles and run before the little kids got there. (I told you she was having a weird Thursday morning.)

Opie found the beetles in a semicircle staring at a white mound on the floor.

OPIE
It's chewing gum.

One of them prodded it carefully with a little foot.

OPIE
Don't, you'll get . . . you're stuck, aren't you?

A BEETLE
Maybe.

Carefully, Opie pulled the beetle's foot off the sticky gum. Then she took off her cardigan and scooped her insect actors gently into it, before making her escape.

About ten minutes later, she squeezed into her seat in double maths, panting as quietly as she could. She had dropped off the beetles underneath a very moist and mouldy condemned building. It had a large garden out front full of big yellow dandelions, and she walked past it every morning on the way to school. She hoped the beetles would be happy and make friends there.

Wood-boring beetles, it turned out, didn't like big goodbyes or displays of emotion, so they had stared at their feet while she thanked them and then one of them told her that he esteemed her. Opie googled "esteem" on the way back, to check she hadn't just thanked an insect for an insult.

She puffed and gasped in her seat, trying to get her breath back. The Slug peeked out of her dungarees pocket. She knew what he was going to say, so she gently pushed his head back into the pocket.

When she was busy opening her books, he popped his head out again.

THE SLUG

You shouldn't really be so out of breath. It was only a short run.

Now this was an unusual quirk of The Slug's. Despite being five centimetres of goo, with one lung, he had immense confidence in his physical abilities. And he *was* strong, Opie had to admit, for a slug. But she did not appreciate being lectured about cardio.

THE SLUG

You need to do more cardio.

Too late, there it was.

OPIE

Shush, please, I'm working.

THE SLUG

Core strength is so important. Look, I can do loads of sit-ups.

He inched out of her pocket and on to her desk. She hid him from her teacher with a textbook. Cillian glanced over, opened his mouth to ask what was going on, then realised he'd rather not know. An invertebrate doing a sit-up is a very weird sight. The Slug looked like a finger beckoning someone closer.

THE SLUG

I'm not even out of breath.

Physical fitness is important, especially as you're a superhero.

Name one weak superhero.

OPIE

Captain America before he became Captain America.

THE SLUG

We both know that just proves my point.

There was a small buzzing in Opie's pocket and she jumped. She'd texted The Resistance her good news as she hurried back from the woods, but had then forgotten to turn her phone off! She'd be in so much trouble if Ms Mollo saw.

The phone was sliding out of her trouser pocket, still buzzing. She panicked.

OPIE
Can you turn my phone off without anyone noticing?

THE SLUG
Ten four.

The Slug was a fan of World War Two films and used a lot of the slang, which Opie didn't understand. She winced as The Slug inched along her arm and down to her phone. He felt cold, slimy and determined. He reached her phone and gently pressed the top of his head against the screen, like a finger. He was very good at using it, although Opie had to wipe it afterwards.

THE SLUG
It's loads of texts from Mulaki.
She says, first, well done, you saved your school!

Opie beamed. As head of The Resistance, Mulaki was the coolest person Opie had ever met and her praise meant the world. She enjoyed this feeling.

She didn't get to enjoy it long.

THE SLUG

Aaaand ... Troy has left London.
He's run away.

"What?!" Opie yelped.
The whole class turned to look at her.

The silence hung heavily. Ms Mollo looked annoyed.

Opie licked her dry lips, affected an intensely interested voice and pointed her pencil at the whiteboard. "Are you saying that if we add *that* and *that* . . ." she squinted to look at what her teacher had been writing on the whiteboard, "we'll, um, get *that* number?"

"No," Ms Mollo said, stony-faced. "*That* number." She tapped her pen against the board with a *rat-a-tat-tat*.

"Ah, yeah, OK," said Opie, nodding as if the other sum would make anyone yelp but *this* one made complete sense. She pressed her lips together firmly, determined there would be no more yelping, and returned to her silent mind-reading conversations with The Slug.

OPIE
What's he running away from?
Varling, I suppose.

Varling was always trying to force Resistance members to join his side. Lately Mulaki had suspected he was after Opie, as she was such an unusual mind reader. But perhaps Varling had been interested in Troy.

Troy was the next youngest after Opie in The Resistance. He was nineteen and worked in the Varling cinema near Opie's house. If his manager wasn't around, he gave Opie free popcorn. Then there was Xu, who was glamorous and sarcastic and twenty-five.

Then Bear and the boss Mulaki, who were both older than thirty so Opie couldn't be more specific. Bear sometimes said "oof" when he sat down, so Opie assumed he was ancient.

OPIE
And where did Troy *go*?

Frowning with effort, The Slug dragged his head up the phone screen a few times. Actually maybe he wasn't frowning, just wrinkling his head against the screen. But he found no more texts.

THE SLUG
That's all she says.
They'll come to see you this evening.

Opie felt her teacher's eyes on her. She stared at the whiteboard, nodding slowly, like she had never considered numbers like this before but now, thanks to this fantastic teaching, her mind was expanding.

No, I don't consider Margot a colleague, really. She's like . . . someone who got fired for gross negligence and incompetence and then I was hired to replace her but she won't leave. Just sits there hissing at me.

CHAPTER THREE

THAT EVENING **O**PIE WAS FOLDING HER LAUNDRY. **S**HE was an unusual, perhaps slightly boring ten-year-old. But not all superheroes are flapping capes and emotional angst. Some keep their bedroom tidy and check the weather the night before.

OPIE
Margot, stop it.
I can see that.

Scowling, Margot the cat lifted a heavy paw to reveal the flattened Slug stuck to the desk. He popped his eyes slowly, one by one, off his stomach.

THE SLUG
No worries, just high jinks.

OPIE
Looks like attempted murder from here.

Margot and The Slug had a difficult relationship. Well, she was difficult. He was always polite. But somehow that annoyed her even more. Margot was not easy company.

Opie jumped at the sound of a shriek from downstairs. She paused, then carried on folding her knitwear. It wasn't that Opie didn't care about her parents – she loved them very much – but they were dramatic about everything. That shriek probably meant her mother forgot they'd bought pears and had just encountered one in the fruit bowl.

There was a thundering noise as Opie's mum ran up the stairs and barged into Opie's room, knocking on the door as she opened it. It was lucky The Slug was good at hiding. He tucked and rolled at top speed into a gap between two pencils, then lay still, looking like a wet eraser.

"Who's got two thumbs and a job on *Highland Docs*?" Violet demanded, pointing two thumbs at herself.

Highland Docs was the soap opera in which Opie's dad Harvey played Dr Ahmed, an ear, nose and throat specialist with a complicated love life.

"I'm playing a flirtatious pig owner," Violet said, striking a glamorous pose in the doorway. "The pig isn't flirtatious, I am."

"The pig steps on her toe and she comes in to see Dr Ahmed, who's covering –" Harvey butted in, having followed Violet upstairs.

"I come in, not the pig," said Violet.

"Not the pig. Dr Ahmed is covering for a colleague. And sparks fly!" Harvey declared.

"Hard to get romantic over a foot," said Violet. "Lucky I have pretty toes. I wore flip-flops to the audition just so they knew."

"In November?"

"I know, looked bonks on the bus."

"Well done!" said Opie. "On the job and the toes."

"And the thing is," Harvey carried on, "we actually need to go and shoot it on location because there's a big car crash in the snow."

"Yes, I . . . uh, nothing," said Opie, who wasn't a great liar despite her secretive double life as a superhero. She had read the script when Harvey left it out one night. Dr Ahmed was going to have a car crash and maybe die. If he died, Harvey would be out of a job (unless Dr Ahmed came back as a ghost which, on *Highland Docs*, was possible).

The big car crash was at the end of the episode, and led to a load of dangerous and frankly unlikely events until Dr Ahmed was lying in a snowy ditch with a broken leg. Wolves were howling in the distance, but he was thinking about his love life. He had a lot of romantic entanglements so this was taking ages. Opie thought Dr Ahmed may well be good with ears, noses and throats but he was rubbish in a crisis.

"So we have to go to Scotland and we were going to see if you wanted to stay with a friend but as your school is off for two weeks, do you want to come with us?" Violet asked.

"It's in the middle of nowhere," said Harvey hastily, before Opie got excited. "I can't stress how little there is to do. Last time the crew were so bored they invented a game called Hold the Cup and it was about who could hold a cup the longest. The production designer won, after four and a half hours."

Violet made it instantly more appealing. "We've got quite a big house to stay in, so we could bring Jackson and Cillian too if you wanted. Why don't you ask them if they'd like to come and play Hold the Cup?"

Opie could imagine how unenthusiastic Cillian would be about that. His parents had loads of money; they were probably going to whisk him off to a beach somewhere. And he'd invite Jackson to go with him and then she'd have no friends for two weeks.

XU
Hey, Animal Crackers.

"Opie." Violet looked at her, concerned. "Are you OK?"

"Mmmyerp," Opie said, which didn't reassure her mother.

It was difficult to act natural when a mind reader had suddenly pushed a thought in your head. Especially if that thought was a rude nickname you had strong feelings about. Violet and Harvey watched their daughter slowly untangle her elbows from the jumper she was folding.

"Ahem, anyway," said Opie. "I'll probably do some homework now."

Harvey and Violet kissed Opie goodbye and left her to it. As their footsteps retreated, The Slug lifted his head up from between the pencils with an excited look on his face.

THE SLUG
Is it . . .?

OPIE
Yes.

THE SLUG
Hello!

OPIE
They can't hear you! Only I can.

THE SLUG
Right, right, right...

Opie hurried to the window to look out at the garden behind her block of flats. It was a pitch-black, wintery evening, and she had to squint into the shadows of bushes and trees to try to see her friends.

THE SLUG
Over on the left – no, no...

He waved his eye stalks around carefully, pointing his eyes in two different directions.

Opie threw out a thought, knowing that her friends would hear it and respond.

OPIE
Don't call *me* Animal Crackers, I just saved my school.

A bush shivered as someone hiding inside it giggled. She recognised Xu's voice.

BEAR
Too right, Opes.

MULAKI
Xu.

XU
Oh, fine, *sorryyyyy*, *Opie.*

Three adults stepped out of the bushes with an air of drama. Mulaki was in her usual business suit with killer heels. Xu was wearing a heavy cape that emphasised his tall, skinny frame. And Bear was wearing vintage knitwear in clashing colours.

They triggered the security light on the side of the tower block so, after a second, they stepped back into the bushes. Still, briefly they had looked *so cool.*

OPIE

So Troy's left town?

MULAKI

Yeah. Varling was harassing him at work, insisting he join his team of mind readers.

Troy couldn't take much more of it, he needed to get away. So Xu –

XU

My friend has a house in a village in Scotland.

I said he should go there and hide out for a few weeks.

He left a couple of days ago.

OPIE

That's such a coincidence! My parents . . . Oh, wait.

XU

Well, dur.

MULAKI

Xu, I swear, if you don't stop being SO rude . . .

XU

Sorry, sorry.

He did not sound remotely sorry.

XU

So we arranged for your mum to get the job
and for the TV show, *Scottish Docwhatsits* –

OPIE

– *Highland Docs*

XU

I don't watch daytime soaps.

OPIE

It's really quite good.

XU

Is it, thoooough?

BEAR

Guys, I'm cold, vintage knits are drafty.

Mulaki took charge.

MULAKI

Opie, we've been working on this for a while. We got *Highland Docs* to hire your mum although Bear was at the audition and said she was very good –

BEAR

She really was.
And it's hard to act in flip-flops.

MULAKI

– and would've got it anyway.
And then we got them to film about ten or twenty miles away from where Troy is hiding.

This sounded tricky, but often all a mind reader had to do was plant a thought in someone's mind and let it play out. Most people, when they had an idea in their head, just went ahead and did it. Like when you think about biscuits and before you know it, you're rummaging in the biscuit tin even though dinner's in five minutes.

OPIE

"Ten or twenty miles"?

Are you being vague so I don't look for him?

MULAKI

Exactly, yes. I don't want you too close to each other in case Varling finds one of you, but I want you close enough in case of emergencies. OK?

OPIE

So if there's an emergency you'll need me to save the day?

MULAKI

It won't come to that.

OPIE

But if it did . . .

MULAKI
Won't.

Opie sighed. She just wanted to feel needed, and like an important member of the team. It was hard being the youngest and the one with the skill that often seemed a bit silly.

OPIE
Fine. But why can't you come and help? Are you staying here?

XU
We're going to Thailand!

OPIE
What!?

She felt very jealous.

MULAKI
It's not a holiday.

XU

It kind of is, though.

MULAKI

Xu!

Opie felt sorry for Mulaki. It was clearly very hard being Xu's boss.

MULAKI

We are looking for an old mind reader friend, Manzoor. He ran away from Varling, and we think we've tracked him down to Thailand.

OPIE

And you have to go, you can't just mind read him?

XU

Mate, Thailand is hundreds of miles away, we can't read minds that far!

BEAR
Thousands of miles.

XU
So I'm wrong but still right.

MULAKI
And Opie, we can't take you with us. You're ten, remember?

OPIE
And useless.
I can only read animal minds.

BEAR
You're not useless, you're the only one who can do what you can do!

XU
It's fun, bit of a laugh.

There was a slapping noise from the bushes. Mulaki

had clearly had enough of Xu's cheek.

MULAKI
You are a valuable member of the team, Opie!

The Slug shivered in the cold air. Opie covered him with her hand to keep him warm. She didn't feel valuable, she felt left out. There was a rustle in the bushes and she knew The Resistance had gone.

"Oh, bye then," Opie said sarcastically to the empty garden.

THE SLUG
I wonder if I should've gone with them?

OPIE
Erm, for...?

THE SLUG
Security. Bit of muscle.

The Slug looked to Opie for her response. She

looked back at him, all five centimetres of brave goo, and inflated an imaginary bubble in her head. This was a technique she practised to make sure no animal (or human) heard her thoughts if she didn't want them to.

OPIE

No, it's good you're here, Troy might need rescuing.

The Slug sat up straighter and looked proud. Opie really hoped The Resistance weren't humouring her the way she humoured The Slug.

I understand you need to feel needed, Opie. But you must realise that you are more than what you can *do*. You don't have to provide a service to anyone, or help out The Resistance, to earn anyone's friendship. You are enough.

Could you pop this down in a notebook? Make notes for me, yes, thank you. It's an important part of our therapy sessions.

Don't write "Opie is very clever and misunderstood". I can read that from here.

CHAPTER FOUR

OPIE MANAGED TO SQUEEZE IN A QUICK THERAPY session with Malcolm the guinea pig the morning before they travelled to Scotland. She felt like she would need his encouraging words to get through two weeks with Cillian being snarky.

He was annoyed because he hadn't wanted to come. She had invited him and Jackson the very next day at school and, as she'd predicted, Cillian was not keen on spending a fortnight somewhere cold, wet and remote, playing Hold the Cup for fun.

"The thing is, Dopey," Cillian had said. "It sounds terrible?"

"No, not terrible!" Jackson defended Opie loyally. "Just not fun at all, in any way."

"My parents are going to their place in the South of

France, if you wanted to come?" Cillian said, looking at Opie.

"What, *me*?!" Opie was surprised but pleased to be asked.

"No, sorry, I was talking to Jackson but accidentally looking at you. My mistake," said Cillian smoothly.

It hadn't gone well, even when Opie told them they were there on official Resistance business, in case Troy needed them. They pointed out, quite reasonably, that no nineteen-year-old ever got into trouble that only a couple of ten-year-olds could get him out of. "They're just trying to make you feel useful, Dopey," said Cillian.

Then Opie had a brainwave at lunchtime. She came up with a plan so sneaky she was almost ashamed of herself. But she was not going to spend the next fortnight worrying about Troy and playing Hold the Cup alone while her parents flirted over a foot.

That afternoon, at the end of the school day, she followed Cillian to his mother's car in the car park. His mum usually gave Jackson a lift too, as they lived near each other.

"Uh, Opie, do you need a lift? Because you won't fit, it's a three-person car," Cillian reminded her. Even though it wasn't, it was clearly a four-seater.

"No, no," Opie said serenely, "just wanted to say hi to your mum."

Cillian gave her a sideways look. Opie wasn't usually sneaky, but *he* was, so he knew the signs.

"Hello, Liz!" Opie waved at Cillian's mum.

Liz responded with an enthusiastic wave. She was always happy to see Opie, because . . .

"Exciting news, Liz!" Opie exclaimed and gave an uncharacteristic skip of glee. "My parents are *both* going to be in *Highland Docs* and have invited me, Jackson and Cillian to Scotland for two weeks while they're filming there!"

Liz put her hands to her face and stared at Opie, her mouth open in silent, intense excitement. Liz was a massive *Highland Docs* fan and Opie was banking on this response.

"Cilly, you have to go and get selfies with all the actors!" Liz was adamant.

Opie beamed at Cillian. "If you're lucky, I'll let you

meet my dad."

"I *have* met your dad, several times," said Cillian. "Last time he was giving out about the bin men not collecting a box because it was *next* to the bin, not in it. It wasn't exactly thrilling."

"Oh my god, what happened? To the box?" Liz asked, like this was celebrity gossip.

Cillian fixed her with a hard stare. "Mother. Please."

So he was in a scratchy mood on the train and for once, Opie didn't blame him.

It was a five-hour train journey to Scotland, but Harvey had promised them they could see the sea for some of it.

"You can see the sea *all the time* in the South of France," Cillian grumbled.

Plus it had been a stressful morning getting three kids, two adults, one slug and a gigantic cat in a dog carrier on a train to Scotland.

They weren't going to bring Margot, but that morning her owner had formally announced that she was their cat now because she spent all her time at their house. Harvey had argued that this wasn't how cats worked. Her owner replied that it WAS, cats choose their families, and as Margot had been draped around Harvey's neck like a scarf at the time it was hard to argue. She had clearly made her choice and the humans around her would have to sort out the admin.

Their carriage was empty. It hadn't been empty when they boarded, but the other passengers had taken one look at Margot hissing in her dog carrier and remembered they wanted to see all the carriages, *you know, really get the full train experience*, and left.

OPIE

Why are you so angry, Margot? You knew you had to travel like this.

MARGOT

I don't want your parents to think they can push me around.

It's important I put up a fight. Now come on, let me out.

Margot made big, round eyes at Opie.

OPIE
No.

MARGOT
I promise to behave.

OPIE
You NEVER behave.

MARGOT
I will just this once, though.

The second Opie undid the front of the carrier, Margot scrabbled out and climbed up until her back feet were on Opie's shoulders and her front paws were on her head. It was painful.

OPIE
What are you *doing*?

MARGOT

In unfamiliar situations, cats like to sit somewhere high, it's where we feel safe.

Margot scrambled inelegantly on to Opie's head, curled herself into a heavy circle and settled to sleep.

OPIE

Can I suggest the luggage rack?

MARGOT
Suggest all you want.

She started snoring.

Opie gazed out of the window and wondered where The Resistance were now. She understood that she couldn't accompany them around the world, but that didn't mean she didn't *want* to.

She watched miles of fields slipping past their train. A V-shaped formation of geese appeared beside them, keeping pace with the train with their powerful wings.

One of the problems with being the only animal mind reader around was that there was no one to teach Opie how to do it. She had to figure out her superpowers all by herself. So a lot of the time she was experimenting by herself.

Now she tried something she'd never done before. Usually when she was trying to find an animal to communicate with, she threw a thought out to that specific animal. But this time she closed her eyes, opened her mind and . . . listened.

At first there was nothing but the clacking and humming sounds of the train, and the quiet chat between her parents. But they started to grow faint. Opie felt her shoulders sink as she relaxed completely.

She sat like this for a couple of seconds. Then . . . it was like someone had thrown open the window of a warm house on a rainy day. *Something* entered her head with a bracing whoosh.

It wasn't thoughts. It was simpler than that. She felt strong and fast. There was wind in her face. She half closed her eyes. It was like she could see without her eyes. If she concentrated hard enough, she could see for miles. She couldn't control where she was looking, though. Instead, she felt like the images were coming *towards* her.

She spotted a train on her left and felt her vision focus. For a second she saw into the train, saw its passengers – a boy staring moodily out of the window, a girl with a cat on her head.

With a start, Opie realised that she was seeing *herself* through the eyes of a goose flying alongside the train!

Her body
twitched, as if
the weirdness was
too much. Startled
from sleep, Margot dug
her claws into Opie's head
and broke the connection.

Opie stared ahead, breathing
heavily as if she'd been running. Cillian
gave her a quizzical look, but she wasn't

sure how to explain what she'd just done. She didn't think anyone in The Resistance could do this with humans – actually *see* what they were seeing, not just hear what they were thinking. This might be something that only she could do.

That was an exciting thought. Maybe Xu would stop calling her Animal Crackers.

She was tempted to try it again, but she was so tired that her cheeks felt hot and her eyelids were heavy. Sometimes doing something very focused with her brain was as tiring as double PE.

As the hours passed, the landscape outside the train changed and became wilder looking and greyer. Cillian watched water run diagonally along the window as the train barrelled through yet another patch of rain.

"I've never been to Scotland before," he said. "Is it a bit rainy?"

Harvey chuckled. "No, no," he said.

"That's good."

". . . It's REALLY rainy," Harvey went on. "One of the wettest places I've ever been and I'm including bathrooms in that."

Cillian shivered and pulled on a third jumper.

"Oooh!" Harvey straightened up and stared out of the window. "Here we are! Well, it's an hour's drive from here, but we're getting close!"

Opie, Cillian and Jackson pressed their faces to the window. There was nothing out there but huge hills, trees growing at sharp angles forced into weird shapes by the winds, and a heavy, dark grey sky. It was beautiful, and a little spooky. Even Cillian looked impressed.

"Their sky is much bigger than the one we have at home," Jackson marvelled and Opie knew what he meant.

The life of a prisoner is hard and boring.
It's the isolation that grinds you down. You
wonder what everyone else is doing outside
in the world, without you. You wonder if the
world will have moved on by the time you're
free, if you'll even recognise it.

Some cats aren't meant to be caged.

CHAPTER FIVE

"**H**IGHLAND DOCS SENT A CAR!" HARVEY SAID AS THEY struggled off the train and examined the scratches on their hands (Margot hadn't wanted to go back into the dog carrier).

A large black minivan was sat outside the station, and a bored-looking driver held a piece of paper that said JONES on it.

They drove for an hour. Their games of I Spy got very dull as their surroundings became nothing but trees, grass and sky. Eventually the driver turned off the main road and started driving along a bumpy track. Opie could feel the vibrations rattling through her ribs. When she looked in her top pocket, The Slug was curled in a ball, his whole head wrinkled with stress.

THE SLUG

I do not feel sick I will not be sick I do not feel sick.

Thankfully there was no slug sick in her pocket by the time the driver turned into a long, narrow, dark driveway. Trees had grown either side and knitted together across the road, blocking out any light.

Opie and Jackson leaned forward from the back seat, eager to see what it looked like. Cillian was on his phone.

"Cilly, don't you want to see the house?" Jackson asked over his shoulder.

"I am, I'm looking at it on Google Earth," Cillian said.

The driver shook his head at Harvey in the rear-view mirror.

The car made a slight turn and suddenly the house was in front of them. It was big, old and spooky looking, covered in ivy.

Harvey opened the front door with difficulty. The inside was cold but smelled nice, like a fire had just gone out. Opie, Cillian and Jackson ran in between the bedrooms, trying to find their favourite. There were so many rooms they could take their pick. They were all old-fashioned, with big, wooden wardrobes and large, lumpy beds. The beds didn't have duvets, but lots and lots of blankets instead.

Cillian was peeling back the blankets on one bed, counting. ". . . four, five, six . . . I'm still going. This bed has got more layers than a lasagne."

There were brown, curly paperback books on the bedside tables. Opie picked one up and flicked through it. The glue on the spine crackled into shards and several pages came loose in her hands. She quickly put the book at the bottom of the pile and pretended it had never happened.

Opie went into one of the bathrooms and ran a shallow sink of cool water. She gently placed The Slug on the edge. He inched his way in slowly, then closed his eyes like a stressed person relaxing in a bubble bath.

"Right, we have a meeting on set in an hour," Harvey called up the stairs. "Are you guys OK to stay here and unpack? We'll make you some lunch before we leave and there's bikes in the shed if you want to go exploring."

Opie peered over the banisters to see Harvey stagger and nearly fall. Margot was weaving an aggressive figure of eight around her dad's legs.

MARGOT
Make him feed me.

OPIE
He knows.

Harvey waddled gingerly to the bag on the table which held Margot's cat biscuits. Once everyone had been fed, the kids loaded the dishwasher and waved goodbye to Violet and Harvey. The door banged shut and there was a moment's silence.

"So . . ." said Jackson.

"Turn the heating up, drag our duvets down to the sofa and watch TV? I'm thinking exactly the same thing," said Cillian.

"Or find the bikes and go exploring?" Opie suggested.

Jackson pointed at her. "Yes, that one."

"It's not safe, the countryside is full of mad prowlers and dangerous people," Cillian said.

"Why do you think that?" Opie asked. "It's not true. You just don't want to get cold."

"Fine," Cillian grouched. "But I'm saying it now in case I don't get time before the screaming and danger starts: *I told you so*."

Margot watched them from the sofa, where she was snuggling under Opie's jumper and a couple of cushions.

OPIE
Can I have my jumper?

MARGOT
MY blanket?

Margot fixed Opie with a challenging stare and Opie knew it would be quicker to go upstairs for another jumper than to have this fight.

There were four bikes in the shed outside, all massive. Jackson gave Opie the smallest one, but even then, every time she stopped cycling she fell sideways in an undignified tangle.

They headed down the driveway, with Cillian shouting things like "We could still turn back!" and "I already can't feel my fingers!" The three of them cycled for about twenty minutes, not seeing anything but trees and hills. Cillian got Google Earth up on his phone and showed them a view of their house from above. They were so far from *anything*. It was weird for three city kids.

"So where do you think Troy is?" Jackson asked as they pedalled along.

Opie honestly couldn't say. Which did make her wonder how helpful she was going to be.

Thinking about this hurt her pride, and so she decided to try looking through a bird's eyes again. But first she had to make sure The Slug was safe. It was unfortunate that Opie had the most success reading birds' minds, as bird ate slugs.

"Can one of you hold The Slug?" she asked.

The boys stared at her as if this was the most ridiculous, disgusting thing they had ever heard.

"I *can*," said Cillian.

"Good, thanks –"

"But *will* I?" Cillian continued. "No, because it's super gross."

Jackson held up his hands and whispered, "Slimy."

Opie looked down at The Slug, who thankfully didn't seem to be able to hear them in the depths of her dungarees pocket.

"Well, you HAVE to," she said crossly. "Because I need to do a . . . Thing that will help us find Troy. And you need to make sure a bird doesn't eat him while I'm concentrating."

"What sort of Thing?" Jackson was intrigued.

"I'm going to get in its brain."

Cillian looked incredulous.

"You'll see. IF you hold The Slug," Opie told them both.

Jackson held out his jumper in a little hammock shape, as a compromise.

"OK, fine," Opie grumbled, tipping The Slug in gently. "But he'll get fluffy . . ."

"Now what?" Cillian demanded.

Opie wished she hadn't lost her temper and been so specific about the Thing. She might not be able to do it again. And now she had Cillian and Jackson staring at her. Feeling the pressure, she got off her bike and walked around, looking up. There was a speck of black far, far away. As the speck got closer, she could see it was a bird of prey: a buzzard. Opie was learning to recognise the different species.

She took a deep breath and tried to relax like she had done on the train. It was a little harder with soft rain drizzling in her face, but after a few more breaths she felt herself relax.

Her ears suddenly filled with the "whoomp" of the wind. With dizzying speed, the bird changed direction. The wind sounds in Opie's ears changed slightly. In the distance she could now see a long, dark blue river. No, a lake – the edges of it were coming into view.

The bird flew closer to the lake, riding the wind with

its wings held out. Now Opie could see a small, crumbling old castle on the shore. The water in the lake was completely still, shining like a mirror. But then something broke the surface, sending wide ripples off in all directions. A moment later it had dived back down, leaving only the ripples behind to prove she hadn't imagined it.

Opie was brought back to herself by a blow to her bottom and shoulder blades. She realised she must have fallen hard into a sitting position, then slumped back. She opened her eyes blearily. Jackson and Cillian were leaning over her, looking concerned.

"I'm OK," she said, struggling to sit up. To her surprise, Cillian sat behind her so she could lean against his back, which was helpful as she wasn't ready to stand up yet. She took her glove off and ran a hot hand over her cold face.

"That bird was miles away, Opie," Jackson told her. "It went really fast, until it was tiny. Were you still in its brain?"

She nodded, feeling shaky. They looked impressed.

Opie told the boys what she had seen. Cillian bent

over his phone again. "I think you were looking at this," he said.

His phone was much bigger and newer than Opie's, so she could see every detail clearly – the long lake and the little castle. Jackson was right, it was miles away. That bird could fly fast, and see a long way.

Opie read the name of the lake: Loch Ness.

"Do you think those ripples you saw were the monster?" asked Jackson, eyes wide.

"Or a big fish?" Cillian was more realistic.

Opie wasn't sure. "Probably a big fish," she said, unable to lie. It really had just been some ripples. Still, she'd been in a bird's mind, watching it fly! That was the most exciting thing.

I saw them forty-one hours ago. Yes, I can
be that precise, I have a very good memory.
There were three of them, one of them in a
lilac cape. It was flapping and scaring the
birds.

Don't suck your trunk, darling.

They seemed keen to avoid people, gave the
tourists a wide berth. I mean, you would
though, wouldn't you?

I can see that trunk in your mouth again.

CHAPTER SIX

THAT EVENING, **O**PIE LAY IN HER BED LISTENING TO Jackson and Cillian chat in the twin room next door. They were sharing it, so long as Cillian agreed to never walk around barefoot. (Jackson didn't like toes. Opie wondered if that was why he got squicked out by The Slug.)

The Slug was sat at the end of her bed, nibbling on a lettuce leaf and carefully pressing his head against her phone, going through Opie's emails. She didn't get many, because she was ten. Still, it was good to have an account for the future. And this was how Mulaki had agreed to contact her while they were in Thailand.

OPIE
Anything new?

THE SLUG
Email from Mulaki.

OPIE
Oooh, what does she say?

Opie wanted to lean forward and read the email herself but couldn't sit up. Margot was leaning against her, solid and unwilling to move.

THE SLUG
They flew into Bangkok and are travelling south, as they think that's where they'll find Manzoor.

Opie managed to prop herself up on one elbow. At least she could see The Slug like this. You didn't need eye contact to communicate telepathically, but it felt polite.

Margot was jolted by Opie moving. She rolled on to her back, pointing her feet at the ceiling.

MARGOT
How very dare you.

THE SLUG
Mulaki wonders if you've heard anything from Varling.

OPIE
No. That's good though, right?

THE SLUG
Hmmm. She would rather we knew what he was up to.

Opie sighed, brooding on how bad guys never stay thwarted. It was quite discouraging. The Slug tried to cheer her up.

THE SLUG

Look, they made Xu look less attention-grabbing.

Opie spluttered a laugh at the photo on the screen. Xu was the most dashing member of The Resistance, and proud of it. He was tall and elegant; he usually wore a long cape and people stared at him in the street. Now he was almost unrecognisable in a slogan T-shirt, sandals and boot-cut jeans. His face was cold, sad fury. The caption read: *Bear chose his clothes.*

Opie laughed but felt a pang. She missed them so much, and their mission looked like fun. She couldn't wait to be old enough to join them properly, rather than sit around and talk to invertebrates all day.

She glanced up at The Slug to check he hadn't heard that, but he was busily sorting through her junk emails.

THE SLUG

Are you interested in an exclusive first glimpse at a new sandwich?

OPIE
Not really, thanks.

Opie lay back on her bed and stared out of the window. There was a soft knocking on her bedroom wall. She knocked back. They knocked again. Opie frowned slightly and went to Jackson and Cillian's room.

They were both in bed, halfway through a hissed argument.

"Opie," Jackson whispered. "Do you know Morse code?"

"I could get my phone and look it up?" she said.

"Should we do that?" Jackson asked Cillian.

"No, cos she's here!" Cillian hissed. "We can just . . . talk normally."

"Right, right, right. Opes, what if we went to Loch Ness one day to see if you can hear the monster?" Jackson whispered, excited. "If there is one, you'd hear it? Monsters are animals, right?"

"Oh yeah, good idea," said Opie.

"It was Cillian's," Jackson confessed.

"We'd have to get a lift, though," Cillian said. "When are your parents free?"

"Not for a while," Opie admitted, sorry to disappoint them both. "They're filming every day for a week, I think. I'll check."

Opie went to her parents' room to say goodnight. She found them giggling over their scripts, trying to learn their lines.

"Opie, we are literally flirting over my toe," her mum said, rolling her eyes. "This script is so silly."

"Sometimes the writers have to work quickly," Harvey said, being fair. "And with writing, you can be quick or you can be good."

"This is *very* . . . quick," Violet remarked, wiggling her toes at Harvey.

Opie felt there would soon be more flirting and she didn't want to watch it. She checked her parents weren't around to drive them for a week, and they weren't. She said goodnight and left them, feeling like everyone in the house was happy. Though, as she lay in bed a moment later, she didn't feel as confident about The Resistance. Was Troy OK? Where was he? What was Varling up to?

And why did Margot need to take up most of the bed?

I tied myself in a knot again. I got to wait for my mum. I don't know how this keeps happening.

Yes, I saw the flapping man and the other people but I can't think about it right now 'cos I'm in a knot, OK?

CHAPTER SEVEN

THE NEXT MORNING, OPIE WOKE UP FEELING COLD AND stiff. She checked the time. It was six thirty, earlier than she usually woke up, but it sounded like everyone else was already up and thundering around.

Opie felt a tiny shifting around near her feet. The Slug had woken up, frozen in a straight line.

OPIE
Are you OK?

THE SLUG
Bit browned off.

More World War Two slang, but at least Opie knew this one. He meant he was cross. She picked him up and breathed on him until he warmed up and resumed his normal softness. Margot watched, and occasionally extended her paw slowly towards him, unable to resist. But Opie kept batting her paw away.

Soon Opie was sat around the big kitchen table with her parents and friends. There was a huge indoor fire in the living room, and the heat was coming off in great waves. Jackson wanted to burn everything he could find. Harvey had already caught him burning a crisp packet and marvelling at the green flames, so was keeping a close eye on him.

"Sorry it's so early, kids," said Harvey. "But we have to be on set for seven. Do you want to come? We can drive you back at lunchtime."

Opie swivelled her eyes towards Cillian, amused. He had been ordered to get selfies with his mum's favourite actors, so there was no way he could say no.

Cillian sighed. "Might as well do it now or Mam'll ask me every day."

"Are you coming too, kids?" Harvey asked Jackson and Opie. "It's fine but I just need to give your names before we get there. Security is tighter, they've had some trespassers."

"Trespassers?" Opie was instantly on alert. "What, fans?"

"Maybe," said Harvey. "Although most of our fans are very old, so don't usually come trekking over mountains to see us."

Opie immediately thought of Varling or, more likely, his employee Max Inkelaar. She couldn't imagine Varling himself getting his shoes muddy.

"Me and Jackson will come too," she told her dad. And she ran upstairs to pop The Slug in her pocket and give him a celery stick to help his carsickness.

The drive to the *Highland Docs* set was long and bumpy, but soon Opie saw the discreet little bright pink and yellow arrow-shaped signs pinned on lamp posts that said there was filming nearby. Since her parents had taught her what they meant, she always spotted them dotted around like a secret code.

The minivan stopped at a barrier. Jackson and Cillian peered out of the windows at the dingy, warehouse-like buildings. Jackson raised his phone, but lowered it again, realising no one would want to see such a rubbish photo.

"It'll be more interesting inside," Opie promised, feeling bad. She should've warned Jackson that this might not be very glamorous. She had visited her parents on set lots of times, and the studios had always looked like garden centres. The minivan rolled slowly on to the lot and stopped outside a row of small mobile homes.

"Here we are!" said Harvey, hopping out and heading towards one which had a sign saying "JONES (2)" stuck to the door. Opie thanked the driver and followed her dad inside with Jackson and Cillian.

The mobile home was very small, basically a caravan without a kitchen. Violet was already there, half hanging out of the window, talking to someone.

"No, yeah, got it," she said with a thumbs up. She looked back at Opie, Jackson and Cillian, who were now all sitting on the hard sofa. "They don't want you three wandering around by yourself because they have wolves on set today."

"Oooooooh," chorused Jackson and Opie.

"And of course, now I've told you, you want to see them," said Violet, looking annoyed with herself.

Harvey had the dubious pleasure of taking Cillian off for selfies with the cast. Cillian had instructions to leave an empty space the other side of the person, so his mum could Photoshop herself in later.

Meanwhile Jackson and Opie were going to meet the wolves.

"They're basically just big dogs, aren't they?" said Opie to her mum.

"I dunno, Opie. Everyone seems nervous about them," Violet said.

Opie and Jackson shrugged at each other. Opie was an animal mind reader, so *she* wasn't nervous. She planned to ask them lots of questions, find out if they'd seen anything unusual.

THE SLUG
Ask them what the trespassers smelled like. I have a super keen sense of smell, we should use it.

OPIE
What a good idea!

Honestly, he was such a good sidekick. She'd make him a little cape if he had a neck to tie it to.

They rounded a corner and saw a rugged-looking man, dressed in many different shades of brown, standing next to a large, fenced-off enclosure. As they got closer, Opie saw that his trousers zipped off at the knee. She hid a smile. Harvey had a pair of those he wore when they went camping. Violet would *always* steal one leg and swear she hadn't.

Violet waved at the man all in brown. "Bruce, this is my kid Opie and her friend Jackson."

Bruce nodded a brusque greeting and held up a hand. "That's close enough," he said.

They stood a metre from the fencing and watched as a pack of wolves paced around the enclosure.

"Are they . . . local?" Violet asked.

"No, there aren't any wild wolves in Scotland. These are bred in captivity."

"So they're tame?" Violet asked.

Bruce laughed in response. Apparently the answer was no.

Opie's smile faded. Something was very strange with these wolves. She tried a tentative thought.

OPIE
Good morning.

She'd decided to be as polite as possible, but there was no reaction from any of them. No animal ever ignored a thought from her popping into their head. Even if they didn't like it, they always reacted. Not these guys.

"Are you talking to them?" Jackson whispered, while Violet chatted to Bruce.

"I'm . . . trying to?" she whispered back, confused.

OPIE
Um. Hey there? I'm Opie.

Again, no response.

Opie concentrated hard and tried to just listen to

the wolves' thoughts. Usually, animals' thoughts drifted out of them like a smell. She imagined Xu, Mulaki and the rest sensed human thoughts that way too. But with these wolves, their thoughts were pointing *at* something, flowing towards two specific wolves among them. They didn't look particularly special, but these two were holding the attention of every single wolf in that pack.

Opie crept around the enclosure, trying to get closer to the two special wolves and talk to them, but she attracted Bruce's attention.

"Whoa, whoa, whoa," he said, giving a little whistle. "No closer than that, they're not tame."

"But you've trained them, haven't you?" Jackson asked.

"I can get them to run in a pack outside and come back to me, because they know I feed them, but that's about it. They're not like Barbara," Bruce said, his face cracking into a wide, affectionate smile.

"Who's Barbara?" said Opie.

"You remember I'm playing a flirtatious pig owner?" said Violet to Opie and Jackson as she led them away from the wolves towards to another enclosure, much smaller and with a little posy of flowers pinned to the inside.

"Mum is flirtatious, not the pig," Opie clarified to Jackson.

"*This* is Barbara," said Violet proudly, and pointed.

Well, look at you gorgeous two, I love your look! Such a darling outfit. Are you a couple? You should be, you look great together. All that dark shiny hair, like a flipping shampoo advert the pair of you!

Can I say, young lady, I have never seen a pair of dungarees worn with such panache, I hope you don't mind me saying.

Oh, bless you, you're blushing!

CHAPTER EIGHT

FINDING OUT THE PIG WAS FLIRTATIOUS WAS THE highlight of the visit. By miles.

They went to find Cillian, who was on the phone to his mum. "I did, I got all of them, look through the photos I sent you!" He was growing tetchy. "Mother. Mam, listen to me. I am not going to ask that old man to do another photo with a better smile. Fine, sorry, 'Doctor Megthorpe'. I have to go now. Why? Because I want to stop having this conversation . . ."

One of the production drivers offered to drop them home. Violet introduced him as Rob. Jackson and Opie thanked Rob, but Cillian, always alert to an opportunity, said, "Could we maybe go back via Loch Ness, Rob?"

Opie felt a pang of panic. She *had* seen something,

very briefly, through the eyes of the buzzard, but she wasn't entirely sure she wanted to confirm it. Also, she wasn't used to Cillian having so much faith in her. It was unsettling.

Unfortunately, Rob was well up for a bit of tour-guiding. As they drove towards Loch Ness, he pointed out herds of cows and who they belonged to. No one asked him to do this and they wished he'd stop.

"Those are Bert's cows, lovely cows they are. Those are Duncan's, I went to school with him, he's horrible. Those are Yvonne's cows, I know some people have a problem with her but I say treat people as you find them and she's always been decent to me."

Opie sighed and stared out of the window, wondering if at this moment they were driving past Troy. Mulaki had said the filming was happening "ten or twenty miles" away from his hiding place. They had easily driven ten miles today already. As the van bounced along rough roads at top speed, finding Troy suddenly felt more possible.

Opie wanted to see Troy. He had always been nice to her, and she was sure he was getting lonely out here. He came from a big family, and she imagined it must feel weird for him to be alone right now, no matter how much he wanted to escape Varling's attentions.

Finally, they reached Loch Ness. Opie got a shiver of excitement. She had seen it *perfectly* through the buzzard's eyes. The lush green grass and the smooth dark blue, almost black, of the loch – she had seen it all from above. She could even, if she squinted, see the outline of the small, ruined castle that she remembered. Seeing it through a bird's eye, she'd felt like she could swoop towards it in a second. But everything was a bit harder when you were a human with two feet planted on the ground.

Jackson hurried towards the edge of the loch and kneeled down to stare into the water.

"Careful!" Rob called from the minivan. "It's really cold, I don't want to have to scoop you out when you fall in."

"Don't worry!" Jackson waved back cheerfully. "I can't swim!"

"How does that make me worry *less*?" Rob was

new to Jackson's way of thinking.

Opie followed Jackson down to the water's edge with Cillian. Jackson put his hand in the water and gasped. Cillian and Opie put their hands in too. The water was freezing, the sort of cold that sends a sharp ache up the bones in your arm.

The three of them fell silent and watched the ripples from their hands spread out across the gleaming still water. Opie blinked. Her eyes felt heavy all of a sudden. She gave a sniff and a small shake of her head to wake herself up.

"Your face went like that before," Cillian said, staring at her. "With the bird."

"Yeah?"

Opie stopped fighting the feeling and the three of them crouched in a peaceful silence, looking across the water. Minutes passed. Opie pushed past feelings of boredom and just sat still, forcing herself to be patient. She was aware of nothing but the cold water on her fingertips and the wind gently lifting her hair.

And then – she felt cold water against her face. It was such an instant sensation that for a moment she wondered if she was going to faint.

She sat with the feeling for a moment and soon worked it out. It was cold water against an animal's face, and she was feeling it through its thoughts. The water pushed slightly against her, because she was swimming slowly and steadily. There was no light around her. She felt like she only knew where she was going through long memory.

These thoughts felt cold and old. Opie had never been in such a slow-moving mind. She didn't really have thoughts, just sensations. She was enjoying the coldness and the darkness and she could feel her big, powerful body moving easily through the water.

Opie swayed gently, mimicking the motion she could feel the animal making. Behind her, she couldn't see but Cillian lowered his knee on to the ground, making himself more stable in case she needed to lean against him.

Opie moved her fingers lightly on the surface of the water. Deep in the loch, the animal sensed her splashing and stopped swimming. It felt unsure. Unlike when she usually pushed thoughts at an animal and they'd have a silent conversation, this was like sharing a brain, with thoughts and feelings meshed together.

Jackson paddled his fingers in the water too, harder. In the animal's mind, Opie felt a stab of fear. The splashing on the surface of the loch sounded frighteningly loud. She felt the cold water push harder against her face as the animal swam to escape the noise, pushing clumsily through weeds. It was panicking and confused and its poor old brain was muddled.

As it swam, she felt the animal's feelings leaving her mind. She sat back thoughtfully on the shore of the loch, feeling a little sick.

"Hear anything, Dopey?" Cillian asked.

"I bet she did," Jackson said loyally.

"If it's in there, we should get a boat and an underwater camera and lower it down on a rope and try and find it!" enthused Cillian.

But Opie couldn't forget how loud even their fingertips had sounded to the old animal at the bottom of the loch, nor how scared it felt. It would be terrified if people started lowering cameras with flashes into the depths to hunt it out.

"No, I . . . no, nothing," she said.

Jackson looked disappointed. They all stood up and wiped their freezing-cold hands on their coats and headed back to the minivan.

"You didn't hear *anything*?" Cillian asked, looking closely at her.

"Yeah, no, probably like an eel I think?" Opie said awkwardly. "One of those big brown fish with the long mouth and teeth?"

"World's dullest superhero strikes again," sighed Cillian.

Ugh, yeah, people swim in here in summer. So gross. I can't stop thinking, what if I brushed against one of their legs?! People are slimy, aren't they? I've heard they are. Geein me the boak just thinking about it.

CHAPTER NINE

FOR THE NEXT FEW DAYS, **H**ARVEY AND **V**IOLET WERE both filming, leaving Opie and the boys home unsupervised. They were quite excited about this, although as Cillian said, it was hard to see what danger they could get into, even if they were trying.

"Which we're not," Opie made very clear to her parents.

Well. Perhaps this wasn't strictly true. They were now determined to find Troy. "But in a respectful way," Cillian had said, with Jackson nodding. "At a distance, leaving him to it once we know he's OK."

They had hunted around the house until they found a massive map of the area. It was a lot of green, and very few buildings, which seemed like good news for finding a person who might be hiding. Opie thought it was unlikely he'd be camping in such rainy weather. Knowing Troy and his city ways, he would take Varling over that.

The plan was to identify certain areas and either cycle to them or, if they were far away, Opie would try to look through the eyes of any bird flying overhead.

"Simple!" Cillian had said annoyingly.

He had a way of making it sound like Opie should be able to do anything with her mind-reading skill, but also it wasn't very impressive, and if she struggled, how embarrassing. Yes, Opie was reading a lot into that one word, but it was all in the *tone*.

Jackson was using a piece of string to measure out twenty miles, according to the scale at the bottom of the map. Cillian and Opie watched as he carefully wound each end of the string around a pencil, stuck one on their house on the map and used the other one to draw a circle around them. The Slug was sitting on the map and inched carefully out of the way every time the pencil approached.

"There!" Jackson said. "That's a twenty-mile radius." He caught Opie and Cillian's questioning looks and shrugged. "I have a horrible uncle who's in the Territorial Army. He made us hike and taught us about maps."

"I'm sorry," said Opie, whose aunt was a fan of long walks in the rain. It was a difficult thing to have in the family.

Cillian was poring over the map and looking at everything in the circle. "So we can ignore all of this," he said, waving a hand over an area of houses near the *Highland Docs* base.

"Why?" asked Opie.

"Well, fine, *you* can go investigate because I'm not going anywhere near them," Cillian said firmly. "The actors are living there."

"Oh." Opie understood. "After all your selfies with them, you're worried they'll think you're following them home."

Cillian ignored her so she knew she was right. "And this is all water, so . . . unless he's on a boat?" he continued.

"But he might be on a boat?" Jackson said.

"Xu said his friend had a remote place," Opie mused.

"Right, but they don't want us to find Troy, so they might say things to throw us off the scent a bit." Cillian was sneakier than the other two so they trusted his judgement on this.

Opie felt guilty looking for Troy after she had been told not to. But then she resented The Resistance for leaving her behind to basically train herself while they were busy having fun on a beach, drinking fancy little drinks with tiny umbrellas. Far too busy to help their newest, youngest member.

Opie wasn't proud of herself, but she had sent Mulaki an email saying: *So I read the mind of the Loch Ness Monster, just in case you were interested AT ALL.* She'd sent it in the morning and had received no reply all day. So that evening Opie tried not to think about it. She just focused on the film they were watching and tried to push all her worries aside. During a particularly loud and violent action scene, she sneaked off to reheat her hot chocolate in the microwave.

"We can fast forward through the blood-splatter

bits if you want, Opes?" Jackson called behind her.

"Oh no, no, I love those bits!" she lied.

"OK, I'll pause it so you don't miss any," Cillian said.

Opie pulled a face to herself in the kitchen and popped her mug in the microwave. As she waited, she stared absent-mindedly into the impenetrable darkness outside. She couldn't see much except her own reflection in the glass.

Then the outline of her head moved, ever so slightly.

Opie's eyes widened with shock. Because she hadn't moved at all.

There was someone standing outside the window. She could see their outline very faintly, because they were directly opposite her.

"Cillian . . ." she called, barely moving her mouth and hoping whoever was outside couldn't hear her through the glass. "Cilliaaan!"

Cillian came into the kitchen. "What?"

"Stop," Opie said quietly, staring ahead and trying to not move her mouth. "Just there, by the door, flick that light switch?"

He must have heard the urgency in her voice

because he didn't ask why; he just did what she asked. A moment later the lights outside the house turned on, illuminating the large back garden and the fields beyond.

There was no one there.

Cillian came and stood beside her. "Is there someone out there?"

Opie still felt frozen in place with fear. "I think so." She pointed. "Right outside the window."

Jackson joined them. For once, he seemed aware of what was going on. In fact, he took charge, probably inspired by the action film they were watching. "Let's go outside and look," he decided, grabbing a ladle as a weapon.

"Ooooorrr," said Opie, taking the ladle off him, "let's be less brave and more sensible."

Cillian nodded firmly. For once he and Opie were in complete agreement.

THE SLUG

What's happening?? Is it danger? I'm good with danger!

OPIE
Stay in the living room, be safe.

THE SLUG
Safety is not my middle name.

Opie, Jackson and Cillian rushed around the house, double-locking all the doors.

THE SLUG
Danger. That's my middle name.

OPIE
I know the saying, please just stay in the living room and be safe!

Opie hurried upstairs behind Cillian and Jackson. She could feel The Slug was moody with her, but she was scared and wanted to get to safety. Plus, she had no worries about the intruder finding or hurting The Slug. Perhaps if the intruder was a big bird, she reflected, then she would.

But the intruder wasn't a bird. She only knew one person that tall, and it was Max Varling.

There were torches on various bookcases upstairs. Opie grabbed every one she passed and handed them out to her friends. They found the strongest three and shone them out of Cillian and Jackson's bedroom window. She felt much safer with her friends on the first floor, rather than all alone and eye to eye with whoever was down there.

Jackson was on his knees beside Opie, a blanket flung over his head, his nose just poking over the windowsill. He had even acquired a pair of binoculars from somewhere.

"You're very good at . . . this," said Opie, gesturing.

"The uncle in the Territorial Army," Jackson said quietly, his eyes never leaving the garden. "When he took me and my cousins out for the day we were only allowed back into the car if we could sneak up on it without him spotting us. He'd sit on the roof and point at us with a laser pointer."

"What a maniac!" said Cillian, open-mouthed in shock at this outrageous story.

Jackson agreed. "He is far and away my worst relative. But I am good at sneaking now. Breathe through your mouths, one of you has a whistling nostril."

Obediently Cillian and Opie opened their mouths. Opie felt sure the whistling nostril was Cillian, but was equally sure he felt the same about her.

"It's hard to see anything out there," Jackson sighed. "Oh, wait, hang on. What's that?"

There was something tiny, moving slowly but steadily across the garden. It suddenly tucked itself into a ball and rolled at top speed down a slope. They shone their torches at it but couldn't find where it had gone.

Jackson and Cillian waved beams of light around the lawn, confused. Opie hung further out of the window, and just managed to pick up some trace thoughts.

THE SLUG
– evasive manoeuvres.

OPIE

What are you doing out there? That's not staying safe! And how did you get outside so quickly?

THE SLUG

Good cardio. And . . . gravity.

OPIE

You fell?

THE SLUG

I fell a bit.

OPIE

Can you see anyone?

THE SLUG

No. There's a smell of someone who *was* here but is not any more.
And footprints!

OPIE
Big?

THE SLUG
Everything's big to me.

OPIE
Of course.

THE SLUG
Think they stood there a while.
I'm struggling to climb out of a footprint.

"It's The Slug, he's investigating," she whispered to the boys.

"Oh good, I'm glad we've got muscle on the case," Cillian said and Jackson giggled quietly into the blanket.

"He's moving a lot quicker than you'd expect," Opie defended her sidekick.

"Yes, because I expect him to be moving *incredibly* slowly."

Suddenly, The Slug popped into Opie's head, sounding tense.

THE SLUG
Opie, I smell a bird. Opie?!

OPIE
Coming!

Opie raced downstairs and into the garden. She could feel The Slug's terror and was scared she'd get out there too late and see a bird flying away with him grasped in its beak.

THE SLUG
Here, here, here! By this stone thing!

OPIE
The BIRD BATH?!

THE SLUG
Waaaaaaahhh! Literally the worst place to be!

Opie dived for him just in time, she could see an owl zooming towards him from a nearby tree. It was small but determined.

OWL
Mineminemine. Oh.

"Sorry!" Opie gasped, automatically polite as she cradled her friend in her hands and hurried him back into the house. She could feel him still shaking.

I really don't know how
this happened.

Right?!
Glad it's not just me.

CHAPTER TEN

OPIE RAN THE KITCHEN TAP AND CAREFULLY DRIPPED some warmish water on to a large cabbage leaf for the stressed Slug. Then she carried the makeshift cabbage saucer carefully to the table, where The Slug was recovering. She did admire The Slug's bravery, but sometimes felt like he would go to extreme lengths just to impress her.

Opie gently picked up The Slug, careful not to squeeze him, and placed him on the cabbage leaf.

OPIE
It's a drink and a bath and you can eat it.

THE SLUG
That's clever, thank you.

He started doing all three things, still a bit woozy.

"So you didn't actually see who it was?" Cillian asked, leaning closer to The Slug.

Opie started translating The Slug's thoughts to them. "No, they were gone by the time I got out there. They must be extraordinarily fast to get away so quickly."

"And how long did it take you to get out there?" Jackson asked.

"Five to ten minutes," Opie answered for The Slug, who didn't wear a watch. Cillian smirked.

"That's very fast for a slug, Cillian," Opie defended her friend. "I'd like to see you travel faster on your stomach."

Never wrong, Cillian got on the floor and started wriggling on his stomach. He barely moved and after a while they stopped watching him.

Opie wished her parents were home. Between her dizzy slug bodyguard and Cillian writhing on the floor, she didn't feel like they were a strong team to tackle an intruder.

She went into the living room and picked up Margot,

who was snoozing on the sofa. The cat lay limp and heavy in Opie's arms as she carried her back to the kitchen, holding her like a baby. She was reassuringly large, though no help in a crisis.

"Maybe if someone saw her from a distance they'd think she was a dog," said Cillian thoughtfully. "She's big enough. Shame she'd never bother herself to defend any of us."

MARGOT
Too right.

Opie nodded. "Yeah, I wouldn't look to her for help for anything *ever*."

"Should we tell your mum and dad, Opie?" Jackson asked.

Opie and Cillian said nothing.

THE SLUG
Should really.

Opie, Cillian and Jackson pretended to think about

it. But Opie knew they would say nothing. They liked their freedom. It didn't feel right, but it would be worse to be babysat.

The Slug shook his head. Well, the top half of his body. But the tone was clear.

THE SLUG
Good thing I'm here to protect you all.

Opie wished she shared The Slug's confidence in his strength.

Her phone vibrated.

"Oooh!" she said, unable to play it cool. "An email from Mulaki! News from The Resistance . . . but that's weird. It's a photo."

Cillian and Jackson bumped heads in their excitement to see Opie's phone screen.

"What's that a photo OF?" Jackson asked, rubbing his forehead.

"I don't . . . know," said Opie softly. It was like someone had taken a photo while falling over. She enlarged it, but that didn't help. "Mulaki says Troy never turned up at Xu's friend's house. And then yesterday he sent them this photo."

"So he has his phone? Can't we just call him?" Cillian asked.

"He has his phone but he's only using it in emergencies as Varling can track his phone signal and find him." Opie read the email again.

"What sort of emergency is this?" wondered Jackson, staring at the photo.

"Brown and furry," said Cillian, naming the only two things they could see in the photo. "It's an animal, isn't it?"

"What's brown and furry and lives in Scotland?" Opie said.

"I don't know! What's brown and furry and lives in Scotland?" asked Jackson.

Opie and Cillian stared at him, baffled.

"Sorry, I thought you were doing a joke," he said.

Cillian gasped and held one finger up. "It could be anything!" he declared. "A bear, a lion, a . . . a . . . hairy walrus, if that's a thing."

"In *Scotland*?" Opie asked.

"Yes," said Cillian. "Because there's a safari park."

"Oh!" Opie was excited. "Mum can take us! She's back late tonight, but not filming tomorrow."

"A plan!" said Cillian, his eyes gleaming.

That night they all took a heavy torch up to bed. Opie slept with hers on her bedside table: a weapon as well as a torch. She knew the boys were doing the same, just in case the man outside the window came back.

Or a hairy walrus, if that was a thing.

Will there be Scottish wildcats at the safari? I'm not coming if there are. I met one once and she was rude. Or I was rude. I forget which. But I'm not coming. Leave the telly and the heating on and the fridge open.

CHAPTER ELEVEN

EXCITED BY THEIR PLAN AND THE THOUGHT OF FINDING Troy, they were up early the next morning. Sadly, Violet hadn't got in until two in the morning, so at nine o'clock she was lying on the sofa with a cold, damp flannel over her face. Filming was hard work, she said. She only had a day off now because Barbara the pig needed to rest.

"Just twenty more minutes and I'll go and shower," she said, her voice a little muffled by the flannel.

Opie didn't know why she was surprised. Violet was notoriously bad at leaving the house. Harvey said if the house was on fire, she'd double back and prune the peace lily.

Opie, Cillian and Jackson played a board game in one of the guest bedrooms while they waited. It was a very boring and intricate game they'd found under one of the beds. After ten minutes Opie was all for packing the game away, but Cillian was winning and wouldn't let her. Or he thought he was winning. The rules were very complicated and there were lots of them.

"OK," Opie said. "So I'm going to move twelve blue discs –"

"The Goblins of Orpeth," Cillian corrected her. The coloured discs all had names like the Goblins of Orpeth, or the Angels of Nawkang, when really the only names they suited were Yellow, Blue or Old Roundy.

"Are you absolutely sure we've got the right rules for the right game?" Jackson asked, not for the first time.

Opie felt a weight on the bed behind her and knew the game was about to get more difficult. Margot peered around her at the board. She raised a heavy paw.

"No," Cillian pointed at her. "Bad cat."

MARGOT
Yeah, I am.

She swiped at the board, and growled as Opie caught it before she made contact and scattered the discs everywhere. With difficulty Opie stuffed the cat behind her, hoping if Margot couldn't see the game she'd get bored and nod off.

They carried on playing and puzzling over the rules. Every now and then Opie would feel a trembling behind her as Margot stiffened up, preparing to pounce. For some reason, Margot always wiggled her bum before she sprang into attack, and it gave Opie time to grab hold of her.

OPIE
No.

MARGOT
You're annoying me. I'm annoyed.

They were so intent on the game that they jumped

when Violet opened the door.

"Let's go on safari, guys!" she said.

"Yes!" Opie jumped up, knocking the board.

Cillian leaped at it and stopped the discs from sliding. "Don't! I'm still winning, I think."

"I hope we find Troy," said Jackson as they hurried to put their coats on. "He'll feel a lot better knowing you're here."

Opie felt very proud of herself.

"Let's not get carried away," Cillian corrected him. "She's not Batgirl. She's Can-Have-a-Chat-with-a-Bat Girl."

They got in the car and drove for about an hour. Opie leaned back in her seat and stared up at the sky, with its clouds of grey, white and brown melting into each other like a watercolour painting. The brown clouds reminded her of Margot's beautiful fur. Her dad once said that the nicest thing about Margot was watching her sleep, as you could appreciate how pretty she was but didn't have to deal with her personality.

She felt a little fizz of excitement in her stomach.

She might see Troy today. She hoped he was OK. It was impossible to tell how big the brown furry creature in the photo was, or how dangerous. But it was worrying that all he'd been able to send them was a blurry image.

The safari park was deserted, as you'd expect for a wintery Tuesday. The woman on the ticket booth seemed surprised to see them.

"Just to warn," she said, handing Violet her receipt and a brochure for the safari. "Most of the animals will be tucked up in the warmth so you won't see them."

"Didn't warn me before I paid, did you?" said Violet bluntly. Opie squirmed.

"I did not," the woman said, equally blunt. "Have fun."

The car rolled slowly through field after field, with everyone staring out of the window and seeing nothing.

"Well, it's nice to see fields?" said Jackson politely. "Oh, look!!" He pointed. "Over there!"

"What is it?" Cillian demanded, climbing over Opie to see out of the window.

"A mouse!" Jackson was pleased with himself.

"A mouse?!" Cillian said. "We've got them at home!"

MOUSE
Well, charming.

Opie shrugged apologetically at the mouse, who glared at them and marched off into long grass.

Violet drove towards the car park. She pulled into a parking space and turned off the engine. "Come on," she said. "Let's get out and walk."

"What?" Cillian was outraged. "No, no, Violet. You misunderstand. That's the joy of a safari. We sit in the car and the animals come to us."

"It's not a McDonalds drive thru," Jackson said, pulling Cillian out of the car.

"But it is! It kind of is!" Cillian protested, struggling. But he was no match for Jackson's long arms and was soon stood beside the car, wincing at the cold.

Violet consulted the brochure, addressing them with one finger up. "Now. It is a cold day in a cold country. So give up on the warm animals, they won't get out of bed today. The best animals to go and see are the cold-weather ones. Polar bears, wolves –"

"Not wolves, please," requested Opie. Also they were grey not brown so thankfully she could rule them out.

"– OK, not wolves. Um, lynxes?"

"Aren't they just catty wolves?" said Cillian.

"Seriously, kids, meet me halfway," begged Violet, clearly wishing she was still home on the sofa with a flannel on her face.

Cillian ran his finger down the brochure and stopped at the first brown animal he saw. He showed it to Opie.

"Let's start with camels," said Opie, taking pity on her tired parent. She linked arms with her mum and they walked towards the camel enclosure, heads down against the stinging wind.

The camels were moving very slowly, humps wobbling with fat. They didn't look capable of menacing Troy. Also their fur didn't look like the photo. One put out a lazy tongue to catch a floating snowflake. Opie wished she could be as comfortable in the cold as they were. She had on seven layers, and not one of them was helping. She was glad she'd left The Slug at home watching a documentary about World War Two tanks.

"Ooh, polar bears!" said Violet, heading towards a big tank of water.

"But they're not brown," Cillian objected quietly.

Opie shrugged at him. "Let's look anyway."

"Maybe he's staying in one of these . . . buildings?" said Jackson, lifting his nose slightly out of his jacket and wincing at the cold. But all the buildings in front of them and on the brochure were clearly labelled as cages or offices. It was hard to see where anyone could hide around here.

Opie, Cillian and Jackson wandered after Violet to the polar-bear tank, looking around for clues but finding nothing. Then they watched the polar bears all dive slowly to the bottom of their pool and bob around.

"What are they thinking?" Jackson whispered.

Opie concentrated. She had never read a polar bear's mind before. They felt a little slow, like cold, rusty machinery.

"That one –" she pointed with her nose as her hands

were thrust deep in her coat pockets for warmth – "thinks she might be having a baby but she's not sure."

"Ooh, exciting," said Jackson and held up his crossed fingers to the bear for luck.

"There's something brown in *that* pool." Cillian appeared behind them and pointed at another tank. "Capybaras," he read off the brochure. "They're brown. And actually . . . kind of the right shape?"

"Right shape for what?" asked Violet, who seemed to be waking up a bit.

"Never mind," said Opie, steering her mum towards the second tank. Then she hurried to the tank Cillian had indicated, down a slope that led to a window looking underwater, keen for answers. She watched little capybara legs trot through the water. They were smaller than she'd expect for something that might be menacing Troy.

She suddenly realised that neither Jackson nor Cillian had followed her. With a funny feeling in the pit of her stomach, Opie retraced her steps back up the slope. She could see the top of Jackson's head, but it looked odd. Very still.

A few more steps brought her higher up. Now she could see that Jackson was just staring at a wall, his nose a few centimetres away from the bricks.

Opie felt a little panicked. She spun in a circle, looking for the others.

Cillian and Violet were stood together beside a bench, both staring blankly into space, their arms hanging lifelessly by their sides. The only sign of life was the occasional cloud of warm breath coming from their mouths.

There was no point saying a word. No one would respond.

Mulaki had done this once to Opie's classmates and she had hated it. It made people look like PE equipment, tidied away to the side of the room. But this wasn't Mulaki.

A man appeared around the side of a building, tall and broad in a suit and tweed coat.

MAX INKELAAR
Afternoon.

Opie's heart plummeted. She immediately inflated

the bubble in her head to keep Hugo Varling's second in command out of her thoughts.

Max frowned, clearly sensing the block. Opie could feel him mentally prodding at the bubble, and caught a stray word – "difficult" – which she knew had come from him, not her. He was learning how to get past her shield, but she acted cool and hid her fear. It didn't look like he realised he'd had some success getting into the bubble. She hoped it stayed that way.

"We can talk like this if it makes you more comfortable," he said aloud.

"I'd be more comfortable if you unfroze my mum and friends," said Opie.

"I will in a bit. We have things to discuss."

He stood next to her and watched the capybaras.

"Where's Varling?" Opie asked. "Thinking of a new way to get my school?"

"Oh no, bigger fish to fry now," Max said, in a way she did not like. "Think he was going to Thailand."

Opie poked her nose down into her jacket to hide the look of concern on her face. She'd have to tell Mulaki that Varling was following her.

They watched a capybara dive slowly to the bottom of their pool and bob around.

"What are they thinking?" Max asked, genuinely curious.

"About food mainly," Opie answered truthfully. "And that one hates that one."

Two capybaras stared at each other across the pool with pure loathing.

"How about you make them do something, like synchronised swimming?" Max said. "Or make them fight?"

"I don't boss animals around."

"No? What about making a load of woodworm pretend to eat a school?" Max asked, silky smooth.

Opie smirked to herself, the bottom of her face still hidden in her coat collar.

"That was clever. Varling's furious," Max said.

Opie pulled her nose out of her coat collar to say, "Good." Then she put her nose back in again. She had nothing more to say to this man.

"Think of all the things you could do, all the new skills you could learn . . . if only someone would bother to teach you. Mulaki and her lot are too busy chasing mind readers around the world," Max said mildly, deliberately annoying her. "They don't appreciate you."

"Yes, they do," Opie said quietly, not sure if she believed it.

"You're probably right, Animal Crackers," Max said, sighing as if he was growing bored.

Opie didn't know how he knew the rude nickname Xu gave her. But it reminded her that she wasn't always treated with the respect she wanted.

Max began to walk away. Then he glanced back as if he'd had a thought. "Just imagine what they'd think if they saw you, fully trained up, with an army of animals," he said. "Big ones, impressive ones – what do you fancy, wolves? Tigers! Maybe a snake around your neck. Who'd call you Animal Crackers then?"

Opie pretended that that didn't sound extremely cool and appealing.

"You could do anything you wanted, Opie," said Max temptingly. "We'd get you trained up. We'd scour the world to find another animal mind reader so you had someone who understood you. We can see your potential," he said, turning up his collar and walking away. "Shame you can't."

Violet breathed in with a sudden gasp. Opie's now unfrozen mum and friends were icy cold from standing still, even for a short time in this weather. Opie hurried over to hold her mum's hands and blow on them to warm them up. Cillian rubbed his eyes, looking confused.

Jackson, as usual, was fine. "This is a nice wall," he said, still nose to nose with the bricks. "Really flat."

You said, "What do you want to do?" You
can't say it's my day to choose and then sulk.

CHAPTER TWELVE

THEY HADN'T SEEN ALL THE ANIMALS BUT **O**PIE WANTED to get home, as far away from Max as possible. She hated having her mind read by a man who was scheming against her and her friends, and the thought of him poking around inside her mum and friends' heads was even worse.

When they got back, everyone hurried to have a hot shower to get the feeling back in their fingers and toes. When she was in warm clothes, Opie sat in Jackson and Cillian's bedroom, towelling her hair dry and catching them up on what they'd missed.

"So . . ." said Jackson. "It was the man who works for the evil man who tried to turn our school into a warehouse?"

"Yes."

"Buuuuuut . . . he's offering to train you up and get you a sick gang of cool animal sidekicks?"

Opie had to fight down her natural instinct, which was to say, *Yes, this is very cool.* "Yes, but . . . no," she said firmly, to herself as much as to Jackson. "It's not cool and I'm not tempted. They do evil things."

THE SLUG
And you already HAVE a sick gang of cool animal sidekicks.

OPIE
I . . . do?

THE SLUG
Me! And . . . Margot when she feels like it and, um, well, Malcolm is very good with emotions, although sure . . . he's not good out in the field, for the action.

OPIE
You're right! You're right. How could I

have forgotten?

The Slug still looked a little hurt, and Opie wasn't sure she'd been convincing enough.

"Well, anyway, I did say no," Opie assured The Slug, speaking out loud so Cillian and Jackson felt part of the conversation. "I just buried my nose in my coat, though," she added, aware she could've given Max a more tough "no".

THE SLUG

Listen, when I feel shy, I pull my head right down into my neck. It's a clear sign that you want no part of what's going on.

He demonstrated, tucking his eye stalks away. Jackson stared.

"Thing is, though," said Cillian. "The Resistance can be a bit *too* good. Especially Mulaki. She won't even use her superpowers to cheat in a card game."

"And that's just like light Evil, really," said Jackson.

"Diet Evil," agreed Cillian.

"No, no, no, I am not having anything to do with Varling and his gang," said Opie, wrapping the conversation up quickly, because she was pretty sure they'd be able to talk her round. Who *wouldn't* want to be trained up, get a gang of cool animal sidekicks and even find other animal mind readers who understood her?

Opie really tried not to brood on it, or feel like she'd given the wrong answer. What if Varling and Max *were* only up to Diet Evil? But she knew she was kidding herself. She'd made her decision and that was that.

Her resolve was weakening as she went down for dinner that evening. Especially as Mulaki hadn't even replied to her email about the Loch Ness Monster. How many beach cocktails could they be drinking that an email THAT exciting didn't get a reply?

Later, as she was eating dinner with her parents and friends, her eyes suddenly widened.

"Are you choking?" Harvey asked, his hand poised over her back, ready to slap it.

Opie shook her head. She wasn't choking. A voice had suddenly appeared in her mind.

XU
There she is. Animal Crackers.

For the first time ever, Opie was happy to hear that nickname. She glanced up at the windows. Xu had to be nearby, to be so loud and clear in her head. Maybe even in the back garden. The more experienced she grew at mind reading, the more accurately she could sense where a mind reader was.

OPIE
Welcome back! How was Thailand?

XU
So sunny. But we couldn't persuade Manzoor to come with us. He has a house on a beach and a stress-free life. It was hard to think of reasons why he should bin his flip-flops and come fight evil in the rain.

OPIE
I'm sorry.

MULAKI
Any thoughts about that photo from Troy?

"Opie, you're dribbling?" said Violet.

"Ah yes, yes, I was just . . . thinking about algebra," Opie quickly lied.

Jackson nodded. "I'm glad it's not just me who gets like that."

Cillian looked questioningly at Opie. She checked her parents were engrossed in conversation, and used her chip to draw an R in the ketchup on his plate. Cillian stared, then let out a sudden loud yawn.

"Well, I am ex – *haus* – ted," he announced dramatically, scooping up the last of his chips and finishing his dinner at top speed.

"You're exhausted at seven in the evening?" Violet asked as Opie did the same. She felt Opie's forehead. "Are you ill?"

"I think it was the safari," said Opie, yawning madly.

"Very tiring."

"Probably would've been less tiring if we'd driven around like you're meant to in a safari," said Cillian, unwilling to let this point go. "But there we go."

Jackson stared at Opie and Cillian like they were mad. Opie yawned at him a couple of times, knowing that would set him off. It's hard not to yawn when other people are doing it around you.

"I think I'll go to my room and relax a little, maybe

read?" said Opie, loading the dishwasher at top speed. She thought that was the best place to talk to The Resistance without her parents hearing what they were up to.

"Good plan!" said Cillian.

"I guess I'll do the same?" said Jackson doubtfully. He clearly knew something was up, but had no idea what. Opie had seen Cillian try to show Jackson the R in his ketchup, but Jackson had just admired his peas.

I know Margot used to be Opie's sidekick but I'm starting to think she is happy to hand over the role to me. She doesn't like doing things or working together with people or listening. She's not a team player, I caught her dropping toothbrushes in the toilet for fun.

CHAPTER THIRTEEN

OPIE RAN UPSTAIRS TO HER BEDROOM, LIGHTLY, SO her parents couldn't hear how excited she was. Cillian and Jackson followed. She opened the window quietly and leaned out. Cillian and Jackson stared over her head into the pitch-blackness of the fields beyond.

Margot stirred on the bed. The Slug was barely visible, buried in her fur. She rolled over, pinning him to the bed.

THE SLUG
Have I died?

Opie dashed back to the bed and wiggled her hand under Margot until she felt the soft clamminess of The

Slug and pulled him out. Margot watched, mildly interested.

Opie popped The Slug in her dungarees pocket and leaned out of the window again. It was so cold out there it took her breath away, and she felt goosebumps tighten up her arms.

OPIE
Are you there?

BEAR
Yes! Bit wet out here.

OPIE
It's always wet here.

BEAR
Spectacular.

He didn't sound pleased.

Cillian juggled Opie's elbow. "What's happening?" he hissed.

"Small talk," she admitted. He looked disappointed.

"What's happening more generally, just about everything?" Jackson asked.

Opie left Cillian to explain the R in the ketchup to him. And maybe algebra if there was time.

MULAKI
Do you think we can come in?

OPIE
I'm sorry, not without explaining the whole superhero gang thing ... which is a lot to get into on a weekday evening.

XU
I'm cold, though. Just ask. They'll let you be

part of a superhero gang, right?

What a question. Opie gave a big, blank shrug.

OPIE
I don't know, Xu. It's never come up before!

MULAKI
Right, well, never mind, we'll just stand in the rain ... Eyelashes crunchy with ice ... but no, no, never mind.

Opie folded her arms. She didn't feel particularly sympathetic.

MULAKI
We need your help.

Opie breathed a shaky sigh of relief. That was EXACTLY what she had waited so long to hear. It felt brilliant.
She played it cool.

OPIE

Oh, really. Is it something only I can help with?

Something that has foxed four experienced mind readers and I need to come to the rescue?

She heard Bear chuckle quietly.

XU

Mate, don't milk it.

Mulaki was more patient.

MULAKI

Yes.

Only you can help us. You are very special. Please can you do that?

OPIE

Yes, I can. What do you need?

MULAKI

We'll be back tomorrow at around noon to pick you up.

Which answered precisely none of Opie's questions.

OPIE

Be careful, my parents aren't leaving 'til noon. It's a night shoot, they're filming a car crash.

XU

Dur, we know. We read their minds.

MULAKI

Xu!

OPIE

Don't read my parents' minds! That's private.

MULAKI

Sorry, he did it before I could stop him.

There was a small noise in the back garden.

BEAR
I just slapped him.

XU
He did.

OPIE
Thank you.

Opie closed the window and turned an excited face towards Cillian, Jackson and The Slug. "The Resistance are back. They need me," she said, and good grief that felt GOOD.

Cillian, Jackson and The Slug cheered, very quietly.

MARGOT
Ugh. Everyone shut up.

Opie filled them in on the plan, such as it was. She was determined to meet The Resistance tomorrow with information and thoughts. So she curled up with a notebook and her phone and made a list of every brown furry animal that could possibly be nearby. Even brown furry caterpillars. Though as Cillian pointed out, if Troy was being held hostage by caterpillars, he was too flimsy for this world and they should leave him to it. "Otherwise he'll only die walking into a cobweb one day."

Cillian and Jackson helped her for a while, though they kept getting distracted by videos on their phone. Cillian played his particularly loudly, ignoring Opie's tuts.

"You know what," Jackson said suddenly. "I think it's a kangaroo!" He pointed at the photo. "Isn't that a whisker and the edge of a long ear?"

Cillian and Opie stared at the photo intently. It could be! Maybe?

Opie was distracted by a firm kick to her back. She looked around to see Margot had lifted her head and was kicking her to get her attention.

MARGOT

I'm going to come. You should have someone there with brains.

OPIE

Are you sure? I don't want you to moan the whole time.

Margot stared at her and swished her tail, annoyed. Which made Opie think that was *exactly* what she was going to do.

Sometimes, Opie thought as she clambered into bed a little later, she felt like she couldn't have assembled a worse team if she'd tried. Margot was actively unhelpful, Cillian was sarcastic, Jackson was permanently confused and . . . she inflated the bubble in her head in case he was listening . . . The Slug was great, but a larger, faster animal might be more useful if they were fighting kangaroos tomorrow.

But still, she lay in bed and hugged herself with excitement. The Resistance was back! They needed her! She hoped her skills hadn't got rusty. She couldn't wait to show them the new thing she had learned to do. Could she do it to a kangaroo? Would it kick her in the face? They looked big and kicky.

And what would she wear?!

Silly question. Dungarees, always. There's no arguing with that many pockets.

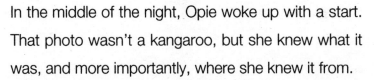

In the middle of the night, Opie woke up with a start. That photo wasn't a kangaroo, but she knew what it was, and more importantly, where she knew it from.

She crept out of bed, jittery with excitement, and hurried along the corridor, trying to avoid the squeaky boards. Then she darted into one of the empty bedrooms. On the bedside table was a pile of old books, their spines cracking with perished glue.

Opie pulled out the book at the bottom of the pile, where she had hidden it after the pages had come away in her hands. It was a book of Scottish islands, which showed her exactly what she was looking for.

And it wasn't kangaroos.

I like it down here at the bottom of the loch.
It's quiet. I like my own company. I don't like
um . . . you know, talking much or telling
stories. I say things like "you know that man
who did that thing" but I don't know the
names and I get sad and muddled.
I am very old and I've seen so many things
they've become mixed together in my brain.

CHAPTER FOURTEEN

THE NEXT MORNING, OPIE WOKE UP BRIGHT AND early – to Margot's disgust. But her parents were already up, eating breakfast and looking suspiciously at Cillian and Jackson. Which was fair enough, as the boys were never up so early or wearing three jumpers at once.

Violet watched Cillian try to drink a cup of tea. He was so bulky with layers he couldn't bend his arm, so he put the cup on the table and lapped at the tea like a cat.

"Are you guys cold?" Violet asked.

Face down in his cup, Cillian answered, "We've been cold since we got off the train," which was believable as he *had* been complaining about it.

Margot came in from outside and leaped on Opie's

lap. Her paws were hard and cold and Opie could smell the fresh air trapped in her fur. Opie buried her face in the cat's side and roughly scratched her up and down her back.

MARGOT

Yes yes. Like that. On the left more. Good, good.

Now my ears aaaaaand STOP, I'm furious.

Opie immediately pulled her hands back. Margot went from "mmmmm scratch my head" to "prepare to die" at lightning speed.

Ready to dash out of the door, Harvey kissed Opie goodbye.

"Now," he said, "emergency numbers are on the fridge, which is full of food. Don't go too far if you bike ride – and Opes, keep your thingy whatsit on."

"Coat?" Opie offered.

"No!" Her dad had the cheek to look annoyed. "Thingy."

"Hat," suggested Opie. "Gloves. Smile on my face."

"BIKE HELMET!"

"Oh right, right, of course."

They waved goodbye to Opie's parents through the living-room window as they drove away.

The SECOND the car had disappeared from view, Mulaki, Xu and Bear emerged from the bushes. It would've been totally slick, except they were all soaking wet and Bear was sneezing.

BEAR
Ugh, Scotland, what are you *like*?

XU
Toot toot! Come on, the car's hidden at the end of the drive,

The Resistance strode off, not a second to lose, leaving the children to grab their coats and hurry behind them, with Margot leaping annoyingly around their feet.

Mulaki jumped out of the car and gave Opie a rare smile. Opie had missed them all SO much. Then she remembered they'd probably all heard that so she stuck her hands in her pockets, looked bored, and said, "S'up."

XU

Dweeb.

Bear gave him a shove. "It's nice to see you, Opie. Have you grown?"

"No," said Opie honestly. She was small and didn't seem to be getting bigger any time soon.

Bear shrugged. "Well, me neither."

"We want your brains not your brawn, hop in," said Mulaki, who had no patience for chit chat.

Cillian and Jackson pushed their way into the car behind Opie. It was a big car with a wide back seat but it was still a bit crowded. Opie put a protective hand around the top pocket of her dungarees. "Careful of The Slug," she warned.

"Breathe out!" Cillian commanded.

They squeezed together and slammed the door.

"When can we breathe in?" Jackson asked in a squashed tone.

"When we get out the other end."

"Kids, do you know the area well?" Xu asked.

They bristled at being called kids, but let it pass as they didn't want to be left behind.

"Yes. There are no shops and it's very cold," said Jackson, helpfully listing everything he knew about the area. "It rains a lot and sometimes strange men stand outside the kitchen window."

Opie felt guilty for not sharing her late-night discovery with Cillian and Jackson as soon as they woke up. But she wanted to tell everyone at once, for maximum drama. She wasn't proud of herself but there it was.

"It's not a kangaroo in the photo," she said.

Everyone gave her their full attention, which obviously felt absolutely brilliant.

"There's a small island," she said, remembering what she'd read in the book. "Ninety minutes' drive from here, called Inchconnachan. It's covered in wallabies after a lady brought a couple of them over as pets."

"Well done, Opie," Bear breathed. "That's a great place to hide. But why did Troy end up *there*?"

"I don't know. But I'm sure Varling is behind it somehow," said Mulaki darkly and everyone murmured in agreement.

Mulaki started the car and headed out of the driveway, with Cillian's phone propped up on her dashboard showing her which route to drive.

"What a relief," Jackson said. "That animal looked really scary from the photo!"

"I know!" Opie was pleased too. "If Troy's stuck on an island, at least it's with small, cute animals. Will he even want to be rescued?"

"Well," Mulaki decided, pulling on to the main road. "I'll feel better when we can check in with him."

". . . scratch a couple of wallaby ears, get some selfies, back home for dinner," Cillian joined in, showing Jackson photos of wallabies on his phone. They really were ridiculously cute: half teddy bear, half bunny.

"He'll want to come back. I think it was just being pestered by Varling that was driving him nuts," Bear reflected. "Bit of time away, he might feel like he can ignore him again."

"Does Varling . . . bother all of you to join his team?" Opie asked carefully, wondering if they had all had the same experience as her.

"Varling doesn't bother with me, Mulaki and Xu 'cos we've been in it so long he knows we're going nowhere," Bear said. "But he goes after the newer ones. Like you."

There was silence. Xu turned around to stare at Opie. Mulaki adjusted her rear-view mirror to stare at her safely while driving. Jackson peered out of the back window to see what they were looking at.

"Has Varling been bothering you?" Mulaki asked.

Opie nodded, feeling a bit hot around the ears. She should've told them as soon as it happened really.

"I didn't think he'd harass a child," Mulaki fumed.

"Yes, I'm disappointed in him," said Bear sarcastically.

"It really is coming to something when you can't rely on the ethics of an evil villain," said Xu.

Bear snorted with laughter.

"I bet he doesn't even check all his recycling is in

the right bin," Xu tutted primly.

"Yes, well, fine, just because people are terrible doesn't mean I can't be disappointed every time," said Mulaki. "Are you OK?" she asked Opie and reached behind her to give Opie's knee an affectionate poke.

"Yes, I'm sorry I didn't tell you earlier, I guess I was . . ." Opie trailed off.

"Thinking about it, of course you were," Bear said, shrugging. "Money's useful. That's totally fair enough."

"No, it's not!" spluttered Xu.

"You've got pots of cash, Harry Potter," Mulaki reminded Xu. "But we don't, and it's OK to be tempted. You said no though, right, Opie?"

"Yeah, yeah, I said no," Opie reassured her. "Just . . . this thing they're filming tonight, my dad's character, it looks like he gets killed and if he gets killed then he's out of a job and that . . . that would suck," she said quietly.

She couldn't say any more as to her horror she was starting to cry a bit and she didn't want everyone to hear her voice wobble. A tear dropped off the end of her nose and into the front pocket of her dungarees.

THE SLUG
Yooooowwwwww ow ow ow!!

"Oh no, I'm sorry!" Opie gasped. The salt from her tear was burning The Slug.

MARGOT
Hahahaha. Brilliant.

Her sadness forgotten, Opie fished The Slug gently out of her pocket and held him up to look at him.

OPIE
Shut up, Margot. Are you OK?

THE SLUG
Hurts.

He never admitted physical weakness so Opie knew he must be in pain. She blew on him carefully to dry the tear.

THE SLUG
Thank you, that's helping.

OPIE
I'm so sorry. I'm always so careful with salt, I wash my hands every time I eat crisps.

THE SLUG
And you're very thoughtful about birds, Opie. Don't beat yourself up.

Opie lowered The Slug to realise that The Resistance were smirking at her.

XU
Can the slimy guy hear me?

OPIE
No, but that's no excuse to be rude about him.

XU

So is he your sidekick? And, second question, very important one, could you have chosen a sillier animal?

OPIE

OK, physically he's an unusual sidekick. But mentally he's everything you could want and you always say you need ME for my brains not my brawn, so...

MULAKI

Good point, Opie.

"Sorry." Cillian interrupted them at this point. "Have you ANY idea how weird it is to be stuck in a car with four people staring at each other and having a silent convo in their heads? At least stick the radio on."

The Resistance apologised. "Just not used to having sponge heads around," Bear explained.

"Don't call us that! It's rude," Cillian objected.

"Is it?" Xu looked puzzled.

"Yes! It makes us sound like our brains just like soak up everything around us."

"And go heavy if we think too much," said Jackson.

Bear made an effort to talk so the boys could be involved. "So what's the little guy's name?" he asked.

Opie was embarrassed. She had never asked The Slug if he HAD a name. And she'd never had to get his attention in a crowd, because of course they were always talking privately in their heads.

OPIE
Slu-Um, hey there.

THE SLUG
Hi?

OPIE
Do you have a name? One you'd like me to use when I, you know, tell everyone about the strong and brave stuff you've been up to?

THE SLUG

We don't identify each other by name, we smell each other.

Opie carefully lifted him to her nose and sniffed him. Nothing.

OPIE

I don't think that will work. Humans just use words.

THE SLUG

Well.

He looked a little bashful.

THE SLUG

There was a word I found and I just, kinda, I don't know, liked the shape of it.

OPIE

Where did you find it?

Opie worried about what this word was and where The Slug might've found it. She really hoped it wasn't a rude word.

The Slug tucked and rolled off her hand like a stuntman and dropped into her dungarees pocket with a soft thud. She watched him rummage around in the corners of her pocket with the tip of his head, looking for something.

He emerged with a corner of a piece of red card, one of those "Sorry we missed you" notes from the postman. He pointed at the top, near the ripped edge.

THE SLUG
I like that, can I be called that?

OPIE
Um, well, it's two words and one is ripped in half, but I don't see why not.

She ran the word fragments through her mind, just working out the best way to pronounce it.

"Guys," she said. "Small announcement. I would

like you to meet my sidekick, Postoff."

Postoff straightened up and pointed his eye stalks to the sky, very proud.

I suppose it is nice to be out of the house. I feel less annoyed than normal. Not happy, I wouldn't go that far. But less annoyed. I'm glad I didn't eat a Goblin of Orpeth, I'd have to be sick by now and people get so fussy when I do it on their feet.

CHAPTER FIFTEEN

THEY DROVE FOR AN HOUR AND A HALF, AND SOON Mulaki was indicating to turn off the main road and down a small track.

"This is Luss," said Mulaki, indicating a small village.

"Looks Nuss," said Bear. Mulaki ignored him though Opie felt Postoff giggle.

"The island is on that loch. I can't see it, though," Mulaki continued.

There was a heavy mist hanging over the loch. It looked a little scary. There was silence from the group. It was clear no one was relishing the journey.

"He's definitely there, right? Just to check," said Cillian.

"No, not definitely." Mulaki never sugar-coated bad news, even when everyone wished she would. "We need to cross by boat, I'll find us one in Luss."

"Caaaaan we wait for the rain to stop, though?" Cillian asked. "My hair goes flat, then my forehead looks big. I don't like it."

Xu made an approving noise, clearly pleased to be on a mission with someone who had their priorities straight.

MARGOT

Me too, I feel slightly less beautiful in the rain though still very beautiful of course. Pass the message on.

Mulaki pinched the top of her nose between her eyes in a gesture that Opie knew well. Her teachers did it when they'd had enough of everyone and everything in class that day. She decided to not pass on Margot's message, and ignored the cat prodding her leg.

If Opie wanted to be Mulaki's number two in The Resistance (and she DID) it was moments like this when she would show her worth. And Opie had a brainwave.

"You know," she said. "I can actually see through animals' eyes now. Well, twice I've done it, but still . . ." She trailed off.

"Like the cat?" said Bear, looking at Margot who was now leaning half off Opie's lap and jabbing angrily at the pattern on her socks. "That's fun. Can't imagine it'll bring much perspective to this situation but –"

"No, it's useful," Opie said, and now the whole car was listening. "I can look through the eyes of a bird flying over that island and look for Troy."

"So we don't have to go in the little boat?" said Jackson hopefully.

"No, we do," Opie told him. "But we'll have a better idea of what's waiting for us."

"Oh. OK, cool, I guess."

"Excellent idea," said Bear. "That's the sort of thing no one else can do."

Opie beamed because that's exactly what she wanted one of them to say. Although – she looked at Bear sideways – maybe that's why Bear had said it. Bear stared out of the window, his face gave nothing away.

"Go on then, let's see you do your thing," Mulaki said, like an encouraging teacher. Which was a bit rich, frankly, as they'd all been out of the country and not teaching her anything . . .

Opie quickly stopped thinking that. It was difficult to be resentful when you were sat in a car full of people who could read your mind and it was them you were cross at.

"There!" Jackson pointed up at the sky. "There's a bird up there! Like a bird of prey, I think?"

Opie was so used to Jackson not paying attention that she was utterly shocked when he did.

"Oh yeah, thanks!" she said, peering up at the bird. It looked like a hawk.

Opie leaned her head back against the headrest and tried to relax. It wasn't easy with Cillian's elbows digging into her on one side and Bear's shoulder on the other, plus a heavy cat on her lap, but she tried. She breathed deeply, in through her nose and out through her mouth and . . . just opened her mind.

Opie kept breathing, trying to ignore the fact that six people and a sarcastic cat were staring at her. Then she flinched, like someone had suddenly blown on her face. It was that feeling again, of cold wind whistling in her ears and a vague feeling that she was strong and fast.

Her vision cleared – though her eyes were still closed – and she could see the village of Luss beneath her as she soared and swooped. It was bigger than she'd thought, and she looked at the trees and houses with their pretty flower-filled gardens.

She thought vaguely about Mulaki's car, wondering where it was. She didn't know how much influence she had over the bird, but the bird suddenly swooped with one strong flap of its wings and flew in a large circle, back towards the others.

There was the car, although she couldn't see any movement inside. Presumably everyone was just watching her breathe deeply with her eyes closed. What an odd thought.

And now, the island. The bird flapped its wings several more times, straining against the wind rather than riding it. It was a struggle. Opie could feel the warmth in the hawk's joints as it worked its muscles.

Wisps of wet cloud made it hard to see, so the hawk dipped down lower. The island was small and the bird was fast, so Opie didn't get a chance to see much of it. She just caught glimpses of trees, grass and lots of rocks scattered all over the ground.

Oh, hang on.

Opie had to wait for the hawk to fly another big circle over the island before she could look again. Those weren't rocks. They were animals. With the hawk's super-acute vision, Opie saw one of them scratch its bum.

Opie giggled, accidentally breaking the connection with a gasp that brought her back to her body in the car. She was suddenly drenched in heat as if she'd been running miles.

"I'm sorry," she said, flustered. "It's made me really hot."

She struggled to take her jumper off but was wedged between Bear and Jackson. Then she got her elbow stuck in her jumper and her wrist pushed up against her face and whichever way she wiggled she didn't seem to be able to free herself. She couldn't arch her back or she'd squash Postoff in her pocket.

She felt Margot slide heavily off her lap and land on her feet.

MARGOT
No, please. Don't mind me.
I'll fall and break my neck.

POSTOFF
I'd catch you.

MARGOT
Lol forever.

Suddenly the pressure eased on both sides and hands were helping her get her jumper off. Opie got free of her jumper with a sigh of relief, only to see her four friends standing outside the car in the rain to give her space.

"Sorry, sorry, back in!" she said, scooping Margot back on to her lap so no one trod on her. "Good news! The island is *covered* in wallabies!"

"So CUTE!" said Jackson, climbing in again. "I'm glad we came."

"Serious question, do you think we could take one back with us?" Xu asked.

Everyone looked to Mulaki for permission.

"Where?" Mulaki said, gesturing at the car. "Troy's going to be a squeeze as it is! Did you see him, Opie?"

"Can I just say," said Cillian dramatically. "I will happily ride in the boot if it means we bring a wallaby home."

"Nice one, mate," said Bear. "Teamwork."

Mulaki pinched the top of her nose again. "Let's just focus, shall we? Did you see Troy, Opie?"

"No, but he doesn't like the rain either," said Opie. "And there was a sort of shack. He might be in that."

"OK, fine." Mulaki clapped her hands. "We need to find a boat."

"And learn how to row," remarked Xu.

MARGOT

On water? I've just decided I'm not coming.

It was Opie's turn to pinch the bridge of her nose. Literally the most useless superhero sidekick in the world.

Cillian bent over his phone to find a tutorial.

I've never been in a car going somewhere
I wanted to go. It's always the vet, and now
this stupid little wet village.

CHAPTER SIXTEEN

"**C**ONGRATULATIONS ON TAKING UP THE THIRD FASTEST growing outdoor activity among people over forty!"

Cillian was playing them a How to Row YouTube tutorial and the instructor seemed unable to get to the flipping point.

"Hurry up, Cillian!" Xu snapped as Bear stood up and immediately lost his balance, flailing and stumbling and whacking Xu in the leg with an oar.

Opie was Cillian's frenemy, but even she thought it was unfair to blame him for that. Cillian scrolled forward frantically on his phone while the boat spun slowly on the lake. Villagers from Luss had gathered to have a good laugh at them.

Mulaki was trying to be patient but every now and then she pointed to the island like, "Seriously, come on, it's just there. That way."

Bear clambered back on to his seat, making the whole boat rock violently. "I just thought, kids, can you swim?" he asked.

Opie nodded.

"I can," pondered Cillian, looking down into the icy black water. "But I don't *want* to."

"I can't," said Jackson. "But I am amazing at floating."

The man on the YouTube tutorial stopped reminiscing about the smell of cut grass on a childhood holiday in France and finally focused on How to Actually Row. Cillian and Bear copied his grip on the oars. They settled themselves on the hard little bench in the middle of the boat and started carefully drawing the oars through the water. The boat moved towards the island.

It looked close but they made slow progress getting there. The boat was bulky and sat low in the water with so many people in it. Plus, Opie didn't like to mention it, but Cillian and Bear were very new to rowing, so every third stroke they missed the water completely, and often caused one of them to topple off the bench. No one laughed though, because they wouldn't do any better, given an oar.

Opie shivered and buried her face further into the collar of her coat. She hoped Troy was OK. She really wanted to just call or text him, but Xu had warned them not to. The risk of Varling using the signal to find Troy was too high.

The rain was still thick and drizzling and Opie's eyelashes felt wet on her cheeks every time she blinked. As they neared the island, she straightened up and pointed.

"Look!" she said. "Can you see?"

"Oh yeeaaah . . ." breathed Jackson, amazed.

The wallabies were forming a semicircle, like a little welcoming committee!

"That is crazy cute, man," said Bear, craning round to see.

"Keep rowing, we're nearly there!" said Mulaki, though even she also was cooing at how adorable the wallabies were and grabbing a couple of photos on her phone.

As the boat drew nearer, Opie thought about what she should say first. She didn't want to scare them, and she was always sensitive about popping into an animal's head unannounced. It was the only way to start the conversation, but it was like letting yourself into a stranger's house and making yourself a cup of tea. And, she reminded herself, these wallabies had lived on the island their whole life, never leaving, as had their parents and *their* parents. Their world was very small. They might be scared of anything new.

"Opie?" said Xu, who'd spotted a funny expression crossing Opie's face. "You all right?"

"Oh dear," Opie said faintly.

Because this had just popped into her head.

WALLABY

Halt, peasants. How dare you approach the citadel?

The boat crunched on to loose stones as it landed on the island and everyone jolted.

WALLABY 2

Begone. Invaders, you will feel our wrath.

OPIE

I'm terribly sorry, I think there must be some mistake.

WALLABY 3

You dare to make eye contact?

Opie dipped her eyes and stared at the ground. "Guys," she said. "Don't . . . get off the boat."

"What, why?" asked Jackson.

"I wanna pet a wallabeee," whined Cillian.

"I – ah – think that would be a very bad idea," said Opie, licking her suddenly dry lips. She held her hand over her dungarees pocket, feeling protective of Postoff.

"Troy!" Xu exclaimed, pointing beyond the wallabies' Unwelcoming Committee at an unrecognisably scruffy-looking Troy coming out of a ramshackle timber house, which looked like the only building on the island. His clothes were ragged, his hands looked dirty, and he was definitely limping on an injured leg.

"Oh my god, guys, thank you! How did you find me? Mind the wallabies!" Troy called quietly as he approached.

WALLABY 3
The human is loud. Chastise him.

Troy jumped as a wallaby bit his ankle. "They're a bit . . . um . . ." he said.

"Horrible?" Opie suggested.

Troy gave her a nervous smile. "Don't raise your voice or look them in the eye or they feel threatened and they do have quite a nasty bite," he advised.

As he came closer, they saw he was covered in injuries.

MULAKI
Troy, what on earth . . . ?

Everyone stepped slowly off the boat and gave Troy a big hug. He looked like he needed it. Opie could hear the wallabies' outrage at their invasion.

WALLABY 3

Sir, their dirty feet are on our beach!

WALLABY

Mete out punishment. Medium strong.

One of the wallabies aimed a vicious kick at Troy's knee. His leg buckled and he winced but didn't react. That was the worst bit, Opie thought. He was used to it.

"I need to get their food ready," Troy said. "Come to my house."

He led them towards a rickety old-fashioned house made of wood. Opie and The Resistance looked over their shoulders at the wallabies, which were still staring at them. One wallaby scratched his ears, flattening them against his face. It was confusing how scary they were, but still adorable.

Troy's house was chilly, with only a very basic stove to heat it and cook on. It smelled of damp clothes and something which Opie guessed was wallaby poo. She tucked her hands inside her jumper sleeves and decided not to touch anything.

"I can't believe you found me," Troy said. He looked so happy to see them.

"Clever of you to send a photo in the middle of the night," Mulaki praised him.

Troy looked surprised. "What photo?"

He showed them his phone. The screen was broken and impossible to read.

"The wallabies tore through my stuff one night and I tried to grab the phone off them," he explained. "Maybe I sent a photo by mistake in the fight. It was completely smashed after that."

"We got this," Bear said, and showed Troy the blurry sideways photo of a wallaby.

"I can't believe you found me, with just that," Troy marvelled.

"It was Opie," Jackson said proudly.

Opie beamed. Dullest superhero in the world, was she? She tried to give Cillian a triumphant look but he was examining his fingernails.

"Troy, how did you end up here? My friend's house is miles away!" Xu asked.

"Varling's guy Inkelaar started following me," Troy told them, while he stripped and chopped vegetables with impressive speed. "He was on my train, not making any effort to hide. It was weird. You booked me that really winding route, which took a few days to get here – train, train, coach, ferry – but he followed me the whole way. I was wrecked by the time I reached Luss, it was like the longest chase ever, and I panicked. I found a boat and rowed out here. It felt like the perfect place to hide for a day or so, and I had food in my bag. But when I woke up in the morning, my boat was gone. Either Inkelaar had stolen it or . . ."

He sighed. "As the days went by I started to think the wallabies sunk it to keep me here. But someone has been bringing me food in the middle of the night and leaving it on the beach. I tried to wait up to see them, but I nodded off every time, after a day of . . ."

He held the vegetables up wearily. "Sorry, I'm talking a lot. I haven't had any company in a while. Big family, you know, I'm used to a chat. I've been talking to a turnip."

There was a mouldy turnip on the counter. Troy had

drawn a thoughtful face on it with pen. It really did look like it was listening.

"Hello," Jackson said politely to the turnip.

Everyone went to do the same until Mulaki said, "Guys, it's a turnip." Which was why she was the leader. Always the voice of sense.

"Max has been bringing you food," said Opie. "He's the only one who knew you were here."

"He's using you as bait," said Cillian shrewdly. "He knew we'd find you and everyone would come here. Now all he has to do is take *our* boat and we're trapped."

That was a horrible thought. They all dashed to the window to look at their boat. It was still there. For now.

"Well," Troy said heavily. "Let me see what blankets I have. I'll try to make you comfortable tonight."

Xu spluttered in outrage. "We're not spending the

night on this mad island, Troy! We haven't come for a cruel and unusual holiday where we wait on wallabies hand and foot! We've come to grab you, get back in the boat, go home, cheese on toast in front of the telly."

Opie nodded fervently. This sounded like a very good plan.

Troy glanced at the turnip as if it was the only one who understood. "*They*," he whispered, and nodded at the wallabies clustering outside, waiting impatiently for lunch, "won't let you leave."

"How can they stop us?" scoffed Mulaki. "They're chunky, sure, sharp teeth admittedly . . ."

"Powerful back legs," Bear said.

Mulaki waved this away. "But they're the height of small children. We can just . . ." she swung one long leg through the air, "boot them out of our way. I don't kick kids by the way, I just heard how that sounded."

Troy shook his head. "You've no idea, man. These wallabies are strong and clever and mean and –"

They all jumped at a banging at the door. There was a gang of wallabies in the doorway and one of them was hitting the door frame slowly with a stick.

"Chop quicker, guys," Troy advised them. "Or the biting starts."

Everyone started preparing the wallabies' meal as quickly as possible.

"This is ridiculous. We have to get off this island," said Xu.

"I've tried to swim it a couple of times but the water is so cold I went numb and started sinking," said Troy. "Plus the wallabies can swim. They followed me out and dunked me."

"They are awful, Troy!" said Bear. "But confusingly, they're still cute."

Troy nodded. "Give it a few days, they get less cute."

"Again – I'm going to keep saying this – we are NOT staying here!" Xu exclaimed.

"OK, lunchtime!" Opie announced, grabbing the half-chopped food and hurrying outside with it. She could hear the wallabies' patience had run out and they were discussing punishment options.

The wallabies bent over their food and started

devouring it. Opie shivered at the sound of their sharp teeth shredding through vegetables, and tried not to imagine what that would sound like on a leg.

While the wallabies ate, Opie took advantage of their distraction. She didn't want to communicate with them as she usually did; she had no intention of pushing any thoughts into their heads. She wanted to peep into their minds and explore their thoughts.

But she'd have to be very sneaky. She would need to employ the technique she used to see through a bird's eyes, where she left herself open to gliding into their mental space.

She tried to relax, but she could hear her breath coming out in an unsteady puff. She was so nervous she was actually shaking. This would not help.

"Opie, be careful," Jackson called softly from the doorway.

"I'm trying to be," she whispered, gesturing discreetly at the wallabies who were thankfully still distracted with food.

"Follow me," said Mulaki.

She crept out to stand in between Opie and the

wallabies. The others came too, and formed a semicircle around Opie.

"What are we doing?" Cillian asked, standing next to Mulaki.

"Protecting Opie. If they attack her, they'll have to go through us first," Mulaki told him.

Cillian's eyes widened. "Nuts to that!" he spluttered.

Opie snorted a laugh. "Cillian, shush, I need to concentrate."

Everyone fell silent. Soon all Opie could hear was the wallabies chewing. As she started to feel their thoughts drifting into her mind, she focused on one wallaby at a time. Their thoughts were all quite similar. The wallabies weren't as strong a pack as the wolves, but they were still a tight unit.

Opie had been in a few animals' brains lately, but these were quite the maddest she'd ever been in. After fifteen minutes, she had heard enough and backed into the hut again. The others followed.

How to explain this? Opie pondered. Well, she'd just give it to them straight and then everyone could interrupt and ask her lots of stupid and sarcastic questions, which she would've answered if they'd let her talk. That was how The Resistance worked.

"So the wallabies have lived on this island for generations, they don't know anything else," Opie began. "They assume everywhere is like here. They think wallabies rule the world and that people are their servants."

"Oh no," said Mulaki with admirable restraint.

"It gets worse. Oh . . ." Opie was suddenly aware of movement behind her. "They're behind me, aren't they?"

Everyone nodded, small nervous nods.

"Can they understand what you're saying?" Cillian asked.

Opie gently read the wallabies' minds. She didn't want them to realise what she was doing.

"No," she concluded. "But they do think we're up to something. Our body language looks like I'm telling you bad news and you're all getting stressed."

"'Cos that's exactly what's going on," said Xu.

"Right. So act like it isn't or they'll get suspicious," Opie said desperately.

Troy pulled an unconvincing smile. Bear copied him. Mulaki wisely turned her back on Opie. Xu and Cillian spun around too, while Jackson did his own thing and curled up on the ground in a little ball. Which was actually quite clever. He looked completely unthreatening.

"So they want us to stay," Opie said. "They're going to eat, sink our boat, then beat us up to break our spirits. They have a very military approach to life."

"It's so hard to reconcile that with how cute they are," mused Bear, watching one of them nibble a carrot. It looked up, baring large yellow teeth.

"Could we outrun them?" Xu asked.

Troy shook his head. "Not without a big head start. They leap really high and land on you . . ." He shuddered, clearly remembering a very bad day.

"Could we fight them?" asked Mulaki.

"I've seen them fight each other and it was vicious," Troy told her. "Plus there's about sixty of them on the island."

"Sixty?" Mulaki was horrified, scanning the bushes.

"Yeah, they're all in there," Troy said quietly.

Opie could sense them now – lots of clever, aggressive brains lurking in the undergrowth.

"They're still cute, though," said Jackson from his ball on the ground. "I couldn't punch one, so if that's what you want us to do, count me out."

"We might have to do a *bit* of fighting," said Opie. "I don't want to but I have no idea how else to get off this island!"

POSTOFF
Ahem.

OPIE
Oh, thank goodness. You have a brilliant idea?

POSTOFF
I do.

The life of a prisoner is a constant struggle.
I fight with the boredom, the silence, the fear
I'll be stuck here forever.

I am completely brilliant so I enjoy my own
company, but this is dragging on.

CHAPTER SEVENTEEN

OPIE TURNED A CUP UPSIDE DOWN AND SET **POSTOFF** down on top of it, creating a tiny stage for him. Cillian, Jackson and The Resistance perched on Troy's chairs and the edge of the table.

"Now," Opie said firmly, holding up a finger. "I am going to translate Postoff's thoughts to you. Please do not interrupt or ask lots of stupid questions or make fun of his idea."

"But we always do that!" objected Xu.

"Yeah, well, take a day off," said Opie, protective of her small sidekick. "Just let him tell you his idea, which I'm sure will be brilliant."

Postoff pointed his eye stalks at everyone one by one, making assertive eye contact. Opie thought she recognised this from a YouTube video about public speaking that he had showed her once. Postoff was ready to outline his plan. Opie began translating.

"So you know when you see a slug on the pavement and then, soon afterwards, you come back that way and you're amazed at how far it's travelled on no legs?"

Everyone nodded obediently. That *was* a thing they had all noticed. Everyone has at least once in their life pointed at a trail of goo on the pavement and said, "There was a slug there just a minute ago!" Then whoever you're with says "Fascinating!" or something equally rude.

"So that's what we'll do," Opie kept translating. "Lie on your stomachs on the beach. When the wallabies look away, use all the muscles on your body to grip the ground and propel yourself along. As fast as possible! And head for the boat. We can cover ground quickly, stop when they're looking, should only take ten or eleven hours."

As one, their audience silently shifted their eyes to stare out of the window. It was raining again, and Opie could hear the wet spattering of heavy rain hitting the stones on the beach. No one said anything, as she'd requested, but the thought of lying on their stomachs for eleven hours in the rain . . .

"And on rocks," said Xu softly, reading her train of thought.

And on rocks. It was spectacularly unappealing.

Everyone looked to Opie to tell Postoff this was a terrible idea. Postoff stretched himself up tall.

POSTOFF
Look, like this!

He demonstrated, rippling the strong muscles across his belly. Opie seized this opportunity.

OPIE
Yes, right, we don't have that.

She showed Postoff her stomach, which was barely strong enough to manage one sit-up.

OPIE

You see? You walk on your stomach, we don't. We use our stomachs . . . to rest plates with sandwiches on while we lie on the sofa.

Everyone else lifted their jumpers to show Postoff their stomachs, some of which were more muscly than Opie's, but none were as strong as a slug's.

POSTOFF

You all need to exercise more.

OPIE

It doesn't matter how much we exercise, we still won't have a body like yours! We're different species.

POSTOFF

You're right, I'm sorry. I keep forgetting I'm much stronger than a human being. That's insensitive of me.

OPIE
Um, yes, well, that's OK.

She felt deflated. "Opie Jones Saves the Day" was not going as she'd hoped.

"Obviously, that's a brilliant plan and I can't wait to die of hypothermia lying face down on a Scottish beach," said Xu. "But he didn't have a Plan B, did he?"

Postoff looked around the room and guessed, correctly, from the sighs and folded arms, that his plan had not been a success.

OPIE
I'm sorry, Postoff. It's my fault. I shouldn't have put you on a cup. It built expectations too high.

Postoff slithered off the cup as if he didn't deserve to be up there.

OPIE
Are you OK?

POSTOFF
Yes.

He curled into a small ball and Opie knew he was embarrassed.

"Oh, hey," said Jackson, who was very kind and didn't like to see anyone sad. "You tried." He went to the kitchen and came back with a sliver of vegetable. Postoff uncurled a little and started to nibble along the edge of it.

POSTOFF
You know, I did have another idea.

Opie was keen to not expose him to embarrassment again.

OPIE
Why don't you tell me first and then I can tell them all in one go? For efficiency.

As he ate, Postoff casually told her his other idea.

Opie's eyes widened.

"Postoff," she said. "That is a brilliant idea. Guys –"

She was cut off by a scream from Troy.

"Jackson, what did you DO?!"

Troy was clutching his turnip friend, which had a sliver of its face missing. Postoff opened his mouth in horror and chewed-up turnip fell out.

"That turnip is not a real person! It's not your friend!" Xu shouted at Troy. "YOU are losing your tiny mind and WE are getting you off this island!"

See! A minute ago I was over there, right?
Now I'm all the way down here. So fast.

CHAPTER EIGHTEEN

EXHAUSTED AND WET THROUGH FROM THE DRIZZLING rain, Opie pushed her fringe out of her eyes. It just stuck on her forehead annoyingly.

They had been working for hours, gathering up branches to make a big bed for the wallabies. This was stage one of Opie's plan.

"I can't believe you're being bullied by stumpy kangaroos, Troy," Xu grumbled. He was in a terrible mood. He hated manual labour; it creased his clothes. "I'm embarrassed for you."

"You wait 'til they attack you. They're vicious, dude," Troy muttered, head bent low over his work.

"Good thing we brought Animal Crackers," Xu said. "Or you'd have been working for them forever."

"Guys?" Opie hissed. "Remember the plan?"

"Right, sorry, sorry," Troy whispered.

Opie slapped a big smile on her face. The others copied her. She could feel the wallabies staring at them. Feeling like an idiot, she skipped over to the pile of sticks, grinning broadly and added some more branches to it.

"I love working for the wallabies!" she cried aloud, thinking the same thing as hard as she could.

"They are bouncy kings and I'm just gassed to be here!" Troy enthused.

"I can't believe I have wasted my life up until now when I could have always been doing this!" bellowed Bear.

Postoff popped his head out of Opie's dungarees pocket.

POSTOFF
Just to check, we're definitely doing this plan and not the other one?

OPIE
Yes. This is for the best, Postoff, because no

one has to lie on their stomach for eleven hours.

POSTOFF
We could be done quicker, nine hours, ten.

OPIE
Still. Oh, be careful.

Postoff edged back into the recesses of Opie's top pocket, avoiding the large, sharp knife she had hidden in there.

OPIE
I don't want to look in there and find you're suddenly in two bits.

She glanced up to see a wallaby hop closer. Immediately she pushed any thoughts of a knife out her head and filled it with loudly, blandly happy thoughts.

OPIE
I AM SO HAPPY!

The wallaby stared at her hard. The look seemed suspicious, but that might have been because she was starting to loathe their horrible teddy-bear faces. It picked up a large stick from the pile and swung it thoughtfully, in a way that suggested it was considering hitting one of them.

"I don't want to get hit with a stick," Cillian announced.

"Cillian, no one does!" Mulaki snapped. "Why do you think you're the only one who doesn't like bad things happening to him?"

Cillian considered the question seriously. "I'm more sensitive than most people, I'd feel it more."

"You can think that if you want, mate. But I'm sensitive too," Bear informed the group. "I'm a butterfly's wing."

"I'm a piece of confetti in a hot hand," Troy argued.

Opie sighed and pinched the bridge of her nose. She saw Mulaki doing the same thing. They smiled at each other, a look of shared understanding that said, *I'm glad I'm sensible but sometimes it can feel lonely in a world of silly people.*

"I think we should just run and jump into the boat," sighed Xu. "It's right there!"

"The only thing is, I've been squatting in the cold for a couple of hours . . ." Bear said.

"We all have," said Xu, still quite snappy (his cape, Opie noticed, had wallaby poo on it).

"Yeah," continued Bear. "And I lost the feeling in my legs some time ago. My clothes are so wet, they're heavy. And I'm wondering how fast wallabies can run? Or hop, whatever."

Everyone bounced experimentally on their haunches. Opie's legs felt weak and rubbery. Clearly they all had the same problem.

"So your plan is to *waddle* at top speed to the boat?" Troy asked sarcastically. "I say we stick with Opie's plan."

POSTOFF
Ahem.

"Postoff's plan," Opie corrected him, but still glowed at the compliment. Troy had faith in her and it felt brilliant.

"We're risking death by wallaby for you, Troy!" Xu protested.

"And it's my greatest fear," said Bear solemnly. "Not death by wallaby specifically," he clarified. "But a silly death where people are sniggering at my funeral."

"This would be such a silly way to go," said Cillian dolefully.

"I guess being harassed by Varling doesn't seem so bad now," Troy admitted. "He never bit me." And he examined a new wound on his arm.

"You need to toughen up. He bothers us too. His number two stalked us round a safari!" Cillian pointed out.

Xu snickered.

"Xu, are you laughing because 'number two' also means 'poo'?" asked Cillian.

"I am, yes," admitted Xu.

This was like herding cats, which was something Opie hoped she would never have to try. She checked her watch. It was late in the afternoon and there had been no food left on the beach last night – luckily for them, given that their boat was there for Inkelaar to see. She could only assume that he was coming tonight.

They would get no warning, she realised, because the mist hung thick and heavy over the loch again and they could barely see a few metres offshore. It was now or never for their plan. As Troy pointed out, here in the middle of nowhere, what was to stop Inkelaar kidnapping them all, keeping them prisoner and making them work for Varling?

"Well, that *is* illegal," Mulaki had said, to a lot of eye-rolls.

Xu shook his head. "Boss, you have to stop expecting evil villains to play by the rules."

Opie marched towards the boat, her hand drifting up towards her pocket.

OPIE
Out of the way, Postoff.

POSTOFF
Ten four.

MULAKI
Behind you, Opie.

Opie didn't need that warning, though she appreciated it. She could hear the heavy thumps of wallabies landing on the wet pebbles of the beach. There were at least ten of them following her, she could tell. She walked faster. It was hard to walk on these slippery pebbles, and even harder to hurry without looking like you were. Soon Opie gave up and started running.

Troy was right. The wallabies were fast. She could hear them behind her, their big, powerful bounds bringing them closer with frightening speed. Running at a half crouch to the boat, she flung herself in, grazing her knee on the seat but ignoring the pain to wheel around and face the animals.

She took the knife out of her top pocket and held it high above her head. Then she flashed the wallabies a huge, terrified grin.

OPIE

I never ever want to leave!

She fell to her knees and plunged the knife down.

Water gushed into the bottom of the boat and it started to sink.

Boreddddddddddd. So bored.

And someone's done a wee in the glovebox.

CHAPTER NINETEEN

"**I**T LOOKED GREAT," TROY SAID, RUBBING OPIE'S LEGS with his coat. "So dramatic."

"Yeah?" she shivered, her teeth chattering.

"Oh, absolutely. Right up until you started drowning and squealing," Cillian assured her.

Unfortunately the knife had got stuck between two planks at the bottom of the boat. For a second Opie had panicked, thinking her plan wouldn't work. And then she'd wiggled the knife frantically back and forth, loosening and tearing away one big wooden board. At which point she'd panicked because her plan was working TOO well. The boat had immediately started to sink, with her still in it.

In the end Troy had had to haul her out of the sinking boat and carry her, soaking wet and shivering, up to his shack. Everyone had now grabbed a limb and was rubbing their coats up and down on her wet clothes to warm her up. Opie felt like a piece of cheese on a cheese grater.

Eventually Opie stopped shivering. Her friends piled wood on the fire to dry out her clothes. Postoff was fine, he assured her. A bit cold and wet were his two favourite states, so this was tinkety tonk for him.

The winter sun had gone down, and it was impossible to do any more work. Opie could hear the wallabies were furious about their laziness, although they all agreed they liked the enthusiasm and loyalty of "the short hairy one". She didn't care for that description. There was a big difference between having long hair and being hairy, but she didn't want to argue with violent, biting animals on a small language point.

They huddled in the shack and waited. There was no going back now, as Xu pointed out in doom-laden tones.

"We all agreed on this plan!" Opie objected.

"Yeah, yeah, but now it's in motion, I think maybe it's a terrible idea," said Xu with typical bluntness.

POSTOFF

He is not a team player.

"You are not a team player," Opie told Xu. "That's from Postoff and me, the creator of the plan and the one who carried it out. And all you did was get wallaby poo on your cape."

"No!" Xu jumped up and spun around in a panic. His cape flared out and everyone got flicked with poo.

So the mood in the shack was a little sour as night wore on.

They were all exhausted but had agreed nobody should fall asleep so they sat there in silence except for this, said repeatedly.

"You're falling asleep!"

"I am NOT. YOU are!"

Every now and then Opie checked on Postoff and found, with a pang of panic, that he wasn't where she'd last seen him. Each time he was halfway up the wall, across the floor or – once, memorably – on the ceiling.

POSTOFF

See! You took your eye off me and then before you knew it, I'd travelled really far. Slug skills!

OPIE

Postoff, I know! You don't have anything to prove to me. We only didn't do that plan because our stomachs aren't strong enough. Now peel off the ceiling and let me catch you.

It passed midnight, and then one and two in the morning. Opie was doing such wide yawns they made her ears pop. Her chin was dipping towards her chest, she was dangerously close to nodding off . . . when suddenly her eyes opened wide. Across the room, Cillian did the same thing.

They had both heard a speedboat engine. Now it abruptly turned off and there was the soft crunch of pebbles as a boat glided sneakily on to the beach.

Heads lifted around the room. Everyone was ready – apart from Troy, who was sound asleep.

"OK, Troy?" said Mulaki.

Troy started awake. His job this evening was to think about a strange Bulgarian film he'd watched once, late at night. He had nodded off halfway through, and woken up to the last half of the film *Cats*. For months he'd thought it was all one film. The experience had been so weird that to any unsuspecting mind reader, he would be asleep and having a dream.

Meanwhile, the rest of The Resistance, Cillian and Jackson were to inflate the bubbles in their head that stopped a mind reader from being able to get into their thoughts, and creep, undetected, around the bushes on the island.

There were four soft crunches as two people stepped on to the beach. Everyone but Troy started crawling towards the back door. Opie looked back at Troy. He was bouncing slightly, presumably to the beat of a song from *Cats*, and gave her a thumbs up.

Opie and the others crept out of the shack and towards the beach, hopping from one patch of grass to another to avoid crunching on the pebbles. The moon was unhelpfully bright. They couldn't see Max

Inkelaar or Varling – who Opie guessed was the second person – but they were listening intently to their soft, crunching footsteps.

Opie heard a strange, sharp *bzzz* above the crunches. Jackson heard it too. Together, they quietly pulled back a couple of branches so that they could peek through.

Max Inkelaar was holding a short, thin stick, the end of which sparked with electricity. A wallaby bounced towards him aggressively – and Max poked it with the stick. There was a *bzz,* and the wallaby shot away from him with a yelp of pain.

"Electric cattle prod," Jackson whispered.

HURT WALLABY
He brought the hurt stick.

OTHER WALLABY
I respect it.

HURT WALLABY
Oh, completely. Show of force. Great attitude.

Cillian and The Resistance were some way ahead of Opie and Jackson. Opie gave Jackson a small prod in the back to hurry up and follow.

Xu was leading. He stopped suddenly, causing everyone else to bump into him. They'd run out of bushes to hide behind, and they couldn't go any further without being seen.

Mulaki made a big, round gesture at everyone with her hands to keep their bubbles inflated. Opie was doing that – she didn't want Max or Varling to know she was there – but she had to stop every now and then to cautiously read the wallaby minds.

She threw her mind out towards the bushes on the other side of the island, where the wallabies sheltered and slept. They were awake and watchful, but giving Max and "the hurt stick" a wide berth. They were clearly used to him, though this was the first time they'd seen Varling.

Max suddenly stared directly towards the place where The Resistance was hiding. Xu nudged Opie, who reinflated her bubble fast. But it was too late. He'd sensed something.

Toying with the cattle prod, Max stepped towards the bushes. He came closer just as the clouds moved away from the moon and shone a bright beam of light at the bushes.

Beside Opie, Jackson brushed against a branch with a rustling noise.

Max moved the cattle prod to his left hand, using his right to grab the branch and pull it down. The action would bring him face to face with Jackson.

Opie did something she'd sworn she would never do.

She shot out a hard, commanding thought towards the bushes where she knew the wallabies were.

OPIE
Intruders. Danger. ATTACK.

With an explosive noise of cracking branches and the scattering of stones, three wallabies shot out of the bushes and pelted towards the men. One of them landed on Varling, feet first on his back, shoving him down to the ground.

"Max!" Varling yelled, forgetting about the need for silence.

Max Inkelaar had his own problems. Another wallaby had launched itself at him, lower but hitting him hard behind the knee, causing his legs to buckle and throwing him to the ground.

Max scrabbled on the ground for the cattle prod and tried jabbing at the two wallabies attacking him. It was clear as soon as he could get them with the prod, they would flee back to safety.

Mulaki grabbed Opie and pushed her, Cillian and Jackson down behind a much thicker clump of bushes where they were more securely hidden. Opie could hear Bear and Xu crouch behind her, breathing heavily.

MULAKI
Opie, did you do that?

Opie nodded, feeling a little sick as she heard the wallabies' yelps of pain. Max had clearly regained control of the prod. This was her fault. She had made it happen.

Mulaki felt Opie's guilt and gave her a reassuring squeeze on the shoulder.

MULAKI
You had to.

BEAR
You did. Thank you.

On the far side of their bushes, there was the sound of someone getting heavily to their feet.

"He's awake," said Max shortly.

Troy had clearly heard the commotion and been distracted from his pretend dreaming.

Varling and Max hurried towards the shack without another word. They weren't bothering to move quietly any more, stomping loudly over the stones. Cillian waved at everyone to follow him, pointing at his ears. They understood. Run while their footsteps couldn't be heard over Max and Varling's.

Everyone ran towards the boat. As Opie got closer, she could see how nice it was, a proper speedboat. It had a name on the side: *Hugo*. Of course Varling had named his boat after his favourite person: himself.

They clambered in as quietly as possible, with at least three of them hissing, "Keys! Keys! Keys!" at Xu.

XU
Why am I suddenly in charge?

BEAR

You're the fanciest. You're the most likely to have been on a speedboat before.

Xu did seem to be rummaging around with a knowledgeable air. Suddenly he was dangling something at them which glinted in the moonlight . . . the boat keys.

Opie started breathing more easily. Maybe it was going to be OK. They just had to get Troy off the island now. The plan was for him to bolt out of the shack and just run really fast for the boat. Arguably the cleverest bit of the plan was at the beginning. Now it was time for screaming and running and falling over.

We're livid obviously. The entire staff absconded, and several of us were shoved, actually shoved! This is the working man for you, always poised for revolution.

We're sending our best swimmers to the mainland. We've never done this before but desperate times call for desperate measures. We've told them to alert the government and hopefully all the human servants will be taught a lesson. It's the only way to rule, strict discipline, no second chances.

Yes, I have hurt my paw. You . . . yes, you could rub it better, thank you.

CHAPTER TWENTY

TROY CAME STAGGERING OUT OF THE SHACK. VARLING and Max were hot on his heels.

"Go, go, go!" he shouted, slightly unnecessarily.

Xu started up the boat. It shot forward, further up the beach.

"No, no, no!" Cillian shouted.

"Well, obviously no, no, no!" Xu shouted back. He had no tolerance for criticism at the best of times.

Mulaki leaped into the icy water without flinching and started pushing the boat off the beach and into the loch. With a lot more flinching, one by one, everyone copied her.

Opie made a noise like "GUGH!" as the water covered her feet and reached up her ankles. This was the second time she'd felt the cold of the loch, and she didn't appreciate it. It was like a hundred needles jabbing into her skin. Her hands were shaking but she steadied them against the side of the boat and pushed as hard as she could.

Next to her, Cillian and Bear were straining their hardest to push the boat too. On board, Xu was still fiddling with the keys.

"Now it won't start!" he shouted.

"Are there oars? We'll row!" Mulaki shouted back.

Xu hauled oars out of a locker. Finally, the boat was facing in the right direction. The water was up to Opie's knees now, and she stumbled on the soft mud at the bottom. The boat seemed to loom high above her, and she was starting to worry how she'd ever get back in when she felt two strong hands under her arms lifting and pushing her into the boat.

It was Troy. He pushed all the others back into the boat too, except Mulaki, who held up a long arm so Xu could pull her in.

Xu and Mulaki grabbed an oar each and started to carve at the water with them. It was clumsy, but working. Opie glanced back. Max and Varling had reached the shore, but thankfully the boat was too far out for them to wade in after them.

Max looked thoughtfully at Opie.

MAX

You made the wallabies attack, at the bush. Well done.

I knew you had it in you.

Any thoughts Opie had about maybe Max and Varling doing Diet Evil suddenly seemed silly. She never wanted to mind control anyone, even these bonkers wallabies.

"Leave me alone," she shouted in a cold, hoarse voice, and turned back to her friends.

She hadn't realised how tense she had been, from the moment the wallabies had formed that semicircle and she'd heard their power-mad thoughts. She never wanted to return to that island again.

"Me neither," said Troy with a sideways smile at her.

Opie closed her eyes, finally feeling safe.

"Uh-oh," she heard someone say, and opened them again.

"The wallabies are swimming," Cillian said.

They were hard to see through the cold mist, but Opie could just make out the tops of some small brown heads, eyes staring intently at them, swimming steadily.

"Go, go, go, go, go," whispered Bear, and started scooping water with his hands to try and propel the boat along faster.

Opie didn't know if that would help, but she was scared enough to try. In silence they all paddled at the icy-cold water while Mulaki and Xu rowed, their faces set and intent.

Minutes felt like hours, but finally there was a break in the mist. To their relief they could see houses – and, finally, the familiar shape of the car. Opie squinted. She could see a familiar face pressed against one of the windows.

OPIE
Margot?

MARGOT

Took your flipping time.

OPIE

Margot, we're being chased.

MARGOT

Protect me.

OPIE

Yes, I will, obviously, just sit tight, stay in the car.

MARGOT

Say please.

Opie despaired of that cat sometimes.

"We'll dump the boat," Mulaki said quietly. "Varling will call someone to come and get them, but hopefully this will give us a head start. As soon as the boat touches land, get out and run."

"Are the wallabies behind us?" Opie asked.

"I don't know. Don't look, it won't help," Mulaki whispered. "Just run."

With a scraping noise and a jolt, the boat suddenly hit land. Everyone sprang up out of their seats. To Opie's surprise, Cillian grabbed her hand and she felt herself half dragged behind him as they pelted towards the car.

Margot was standing in the driver's seat, her paws on the steering wheel, swishing her thick bushy tail back and forth. There was a crashing noise in the undergrowth behind them that made Opie jump, but –

MULAKI
Don't look behind you.

Xu clicked the car keys to unlock the car. The boot sprang open.

"Wrong button!" Mulaki shouted.

"Sorry, sorry, oh god!" Xu yelped, uncharacteristically flustered, clicking the other button.

Bear wrenched open the back door and shoved the kids inside. Opie just had time to grab Margot off the front seat before Mulaki sat on her. She squeezed her too hard and got an indignant squeak. The moment they were all in, Mulaki started the car and Opie felt the wheels spin on loose gravel.

There was a freezing-wet draught on the back of Opie's head as they raced away. She knelt up on the seat to help Bear pull the boot closed. It was really difficult to do from inside the car, and she twisted back to sit down with aching arms. What a day.

They sat in an exhausted silence, listening to the wind howl outside. It started to snow – big, raggedy clumps like the sky was being ripped up and scattered.

"Weeeeeird," said Jackson, admiring it.

It was hard to see anything. The sky was thick with snow. So was the ground. And when you couldn't tell those two apart, you were in trouble.

"Do you think your dad is still filming in this?" asked Cillian.

"I hope not," Opie fretted. "But then I don't want them back early and finding out we're not home." Her parents were meant to film night scenes until the early hours of the morning, but if the weather was this bad, they might quit early and be back sooner than expected.

Mulaki was leaning over the wheel, desperately trying to see the road ahead. Her passengers "helped" by shouting out anything they could see, but she got snappy and they soon fell silent.

"Still really snowing," said Troy, breaking the awkward quiet in the car.

"Mmm," said Mulaki tersely.

"Big bits," said Xu.

Just when you thought Mulaki was in a bad mood for the rest of the day, she'd realise and pull herself out of it. She was good like that.

"A successful day, though," she said, catching Opie's eye in the rear-view mirror and smiling at her. "Thanks to Postoff and Opie."

"Yes, thank you, Postoff," said Opie sleepily, patting her dungarees pocket.

Everyone murmured their thanks. Opie could've sworn Postoff blushed a little pink. Jealous, Margot punched Opie's pocket, missing the slug and only succeeding in winding Opie.

MARGOT
Whoops.

"And we all helped," gasped Opie loyally.

"Except Troy, who was the chump who got outwitted by marsupials," said Bear, making everyone laugh.

"Oi!" protested Troy. "I managed to evade Inkelaar actually, in the shack."

"How?"

"I hid behind the sofa."

"Well done. Really, we should see if MI6 are recruiting."

There was another tired silence.

"I pushed over a really big one, did you see?" Jackson said, and everyone congratulated him. "I felt bad, he was so round and cute."

"Jackson, they were evil!" spluttered Cillian.

"Oh right, yeah, yeah," murmured Jackson vaguely, and Opie wondered if he'd always remember this holiday as the one where he'd cruelly pushed over a wallaby for no reason.

"Ah," Mulaki murmured, sounding relieved.

She had found the main road. Now the tyres ran with a smoother sound and sensation. Almost instantly, Opie's eyes and head grew heavy, and she nodded off to sleep.

She was woken by Cillian clutching her shoulder with a tight, panicked squeeze.

"What?" she whispered.

"Wolves," Cillian said, eyes wide with fear.

Opie could hear it now, the howling of wolves in the distance.

"Didn't Bruce say there weren't any wild wolves?" she said.

There was another howl.

"Well, he's wrong, clearly," hissed Cillian. "Stupid man and his little zippy trousers."

Everyone in the car was scared, looking around them.

"They couldn't get to us, could they?" Opie said quietly.

POSTOFF
Fabric roof.

Troy also pointed at the fabric roof, then made a slashing claw motion with his hand. Opie understood.

"Could we send the cat off to get a rescue team?" said Cillian. "Like one of those St Bernard dogs up a mountain?"

MARGOT

They use dogs not cats for that, because a cat would literally never.

"Can I shock you?" Opie asked sarcastically. "She's not up for that."

There was another howl. It sounded closer this time.

"Just keep driving, fast fast," said Jackson.

"Unless we're driving towards them," Troy said.

Mulaki threw her hands up in exasperation.

"I'm sorry but we might be!" said Troy.

"I don't know where we are!" Mulaki exclaimed. "I can't see more than a metre in front of the car."

"Can you do your thing?" Cillian asked Opie, tapping his head.

"I don't think so," Opie said. "Remember the wolves at *Highland Docs*? They wouldn't listen to me at all. I looked it up when I got back. The wolves only listened to the alpha male and female and they wouldn't listen to me."

"How hard did you try?" Mulaki asked.

"I swear I tried so hard. It's like they didn't even know I was there."

Jackson squeezed Opie's arm. She squeezed him back. She was scared too. She could already feel the jolt of the car as the first wolf leaped on the roof and the noise the roof would make as its sharp teeth tore through it, exposing them all to attack.

"I'm covered in fear sweat," Cillian grumbled. "And now it's drying and making me even colder."

"Me too." Bear patted his jumper under the arms. "Vintage knits, they just don't *breathe*. Do I smell? You'd tell me if I smelled?"

"No, you don't smell, and no, no one would tell you if you did," Mulaki informed him.

"I would," Xu piped up.

The wolves howled again. Everyone stared out of

the windows, trying to see how close danger was.

"Hang on!" Opie cried suddenly. "Bruce *did* say there weren't any wild wolves in Scotland."

"Uh . . . then what's that?" said Cillian, pointing at the window, where they could hear the wolves howling again.

"The *Highland Docs* wolves!" Opie said in triumph.

At exactly that moment, a bright orange barricade appeared out of nowhere in front of them and the car crashed through it. Mulaki slammed on the brakes. The car skidded and slid on the snow but eventually came to a halt. Faces, barely visible in thick anoraks with the hood up, peered curiously into their car.

Opie recognised one of the faces.

"Dad!" she shouted.

She scrambled across Jackson and Bear and opened the car door. The howling cold hit her like a slap as she flung herself at her dad for a big hug. She felt so relieved – and finally safe.

"Opie, why aren't you at home?!" Harvey said.

And she realised she was now in quite a lot of trouble.

"Well," she said, trying to work out how to explain any of it.

The cast and crew of *Highland Docs* stared at her. A lot of them were holding clipboards, which made her feel even more in trouble, somehow. Behind her, she heard her friends get out of the car and give everyone bashful waves.

Now the fear was leaving Opie, she felt utterly drained, like a whizzed-out balloon. But she had to tell her dad what had happened. While she spoke, a scruffy woman with a lot of hair started scribbling notes on her clipboard.

EPILOGUE

"**S**o . . . **wait, I don't understand,**" **Jackson said** for the second time.

"Shush, shush, it's beginning again," said Violet, bustling in from the kitchen with snacks as the adverts ended.

They were watching the latest episode of *Highland Docs*, the one they'd been filming when Mulaki had accidentally ploughed her car into the middle of it. Harvey had been filming his death scene when Opie had shot out of the car and started telling an extraordinary story of an island controlled by power-mad wallabies.

"Those aren't wallabies," said Cillian, pointing at the screen.

"No," said Violet knowledgeably. "They looked too

cute on camera, so the director went with kangaroos."

Opie stared at the TV, her head on one side. Her dad was having a realistic-looking fist fight with a kangaroo that she could believe was real if Harvey hadn't sent her footage of him punching a kangaroo puppet.

"There's me! And Barbara!" said Violet, pointing at the screen as she and a pig ran past.

"The pig's great, isn't she? The camera loves her," Harvey mused.

"Pure charisma," Cillian agreed.

There was a chilly pause and everyone rushed to assure Violet that, of course, she was excellent too.

"So the evil kangaroos want to control the internet?" Opie said, struggling a bit with the plot. "That wasn't what I said."

"No, well, it was very windy so Natalie the writer didn't catch everything you said," said Harvey.

"She could've asked?" said Opie a little crossly.

"Well, when she gets an idea in her head she's off really . . ."

The episode ended with Harvey

and Violet kissing passionately while Barbara the pig held back a gang of kangaroos with a withering stare.

"The main thing is Dr Ahmed survived the car crash once they realised they wanted him to come and rescue me from an island of kangaroos," said Violet. "And that's not a sentence you get to say every day."

Opie nodded. She would not criticise this bonkers storyline as it meant her dad still had a job. A successful end to two weeks in Scotland, all in all. Her bruises

from the wallabies were starting to fade too. Though Cillian still had a bite mark on his leg that he liked to roll his trouser leg up and stare at to make Opie feel bad.

She did feel bad! They wouldn't have had to fight crazed marsupials if they'd gone on *his* holiday to the South of France. But this is what you got when you were friends with an animal mind reader.

Now they were back in London, Harvey and Violet were trying to stay angry at Opie for betraying their trust and sneaking out to have a dangerous adventure. But Mulaki and Opie had decided the only answer was to tell her parents the truth about her mind-reading abilities.

Opie had always thought her parents were very open-minded, believing in ghosts and horoscopes. Her mother had a few crystals around the place. So she was surprised by how sceptical they were about this. She had to mind-read Postoff and Margot, showing her parents undeniable proof that they were communicating with each other.

But once they believed her, they were so excited and were constantly dashing to the window to point at a bird and ask what it was thinking.

This excitement was hard to combine with the stern attitude needed to keep a ten-year-old grounded. It was like holding a bunch of balloons while trying to have a fight. It felt silly.

Plus Harvey had really bonded with Postoff. He was definitely a better addition to the family than Margot. Harvey and Postoff would sit and read a book in the evening, with Postoff using his sticky little head to turn the pages.

It felt like an excellent conclusion to a cold, wet and occasionally dull holiday. The only small snag, Mulaki had warned Opie, was that her heroics on the island meant that Varling would be even more keen to recruit her.

MULAKI

You need to be less brilliant, Opes. Tone it down a bit.

Opie had blushed with pleasure to hear that. And it wasn't even squashed by sarcasm from Xu.

XU

All right, boss, calm down. The slimy guy had most of the good ideas.

Troy seemed to be recovering well. His injuries were healing, though he flinched at any noise that sounded like the padding of a wallaby's feet so his family couldn't walk around barefoot.

Opie doodled on her notebook. *Opie Jones, Animal Mind Reader*. It looked good. She added some paw prints. Then she thought about Cillian's cunning and the skills Jackson had learned from his awful uncle. She couldn't have done this without them.

POSTOFF

Ahem.

OPIE

I am so sorry. Or, of course, without you. Of course!

She carefully drew Postoff, curled inside the O.

OPIE
Superhero slug.

THE END

I liked the bit when the man, the younger one, did that thing with the . . . you know, the bouncy um.

Bouncy um.

Wallabies! That's the word.

I can't believe you wrote about me getting my trunk in a knot. So embarrassing.

Oh, wait, it's in a knot again.

ACKNOWLEDGEMENTS

I wrote this book while cooped up in my house during a very dark, wet January. So thank you to my friends who brightened my days with texts, calls, videos, visits and post: Yasmine Akram, Lu Corfield, Claire McGowan, Beth O'Brien, Hannah Berry George, Caroline Jones, Alicia MacDonald, Kate Quine, Marianne Moore, Chloe Morgan, Emma Eden and the collective known as Tooty Fruity.

Thanks to my parents, Gaynor and Gustaaf, especially as Margot Von Catton now lives with you and is the obstreperous nightmare portrayed in this book. Sorry about all the maimed mice and the attitude.

I'm always grateful to Diarmuid Hughes and Vincent Kearney who were so encouraging when I told them about this idea years ago. Especially as I bet I was talking over the TV at the time.

Thanks always to my literary agent, Hellie Ogden, and Kirsty Gordon, Ma'suma Amiri and Will Francis at Janklow and Nesbit, you are good people and I appreciate you!

Likewise my thanks to the team at Farshore, especially Liz Bankes and Asmaa Isse, and of course my wonderful illustrator Fay Austin who brings approximately a hundred characters to life every book and does it perfectly.

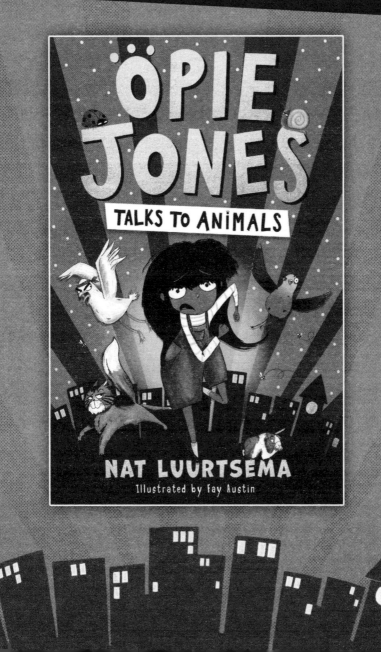

CHECK OUT BOOK ONE!

ÖPIE JONES

TALKS TO ANIMALS

NAT LUURTSEMA

Illustrated by Fay Austin

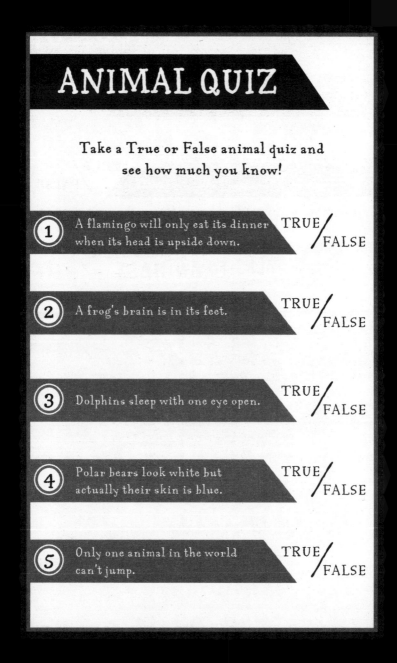

ANIMAL QUIZ

Take a True or False animal quiz and
see how much you know!

1. A flamingo will only eat its dinner
when its head is upside down. — TRUE/FALSE

2. A frog's brain is in its feet. — TRUE/FALSE

3. Dolphins sleep with one eye open. — TRUE/FALSE

4. Polar bears look white but
actually their skin is blue. — TRUE/FALSE

5. Only one animal in the world
can't jump. — TRUE/FALSE

6 Snails' teeth are on their tongues. TRUE/FALSE

7 A koala can survive up to two years without food. TRUE/FALSE

8 Ants love a little nap at around four every afternoon. TRUE/FALSE

9 Cats don't miaow at each other, they only do it at humans. TRUE/FALSE

10 Kangaroos can't walk backwards. TRUE/FALSE

Turn over for the answers . . .

ANSWERS...

1. TRUE
2. FALSE
3. TRUE
4. FALSE
5. TRUE – the elephant
6. TRUE
7. FALSE – but a tarantula spider can
8. FALSE – in fact they NEVER sleep
9. TRUE
10. TRUE

If you scored more than 6 correct answers CONGRATULATIONS you are an honorary member of The Resistance and Opie will be glad of your help. Please hold this slug for just a second.

If you got fewer than 6 questions right you are not yet ready to be a member of The Resistance. If you're disappointed, remember these superheroes can be super rude and their secret missions often involve getting cold, wet and bored. And they NEVER remember to bring a packed lunch.